Praise for

"Relatable and realistic. ⌐____ ___ ___ ͻ
A fantastic debut novel that is unique in the
women loving women genre. I hope Emma
Wallis will continue to produce stories like this."
- Carol Hutchinson, LESBIreviewed

"Emma Wallis writes about difficult topics, and
does so beautifully."
- Emma Nichols, Author

"Emma Wallis is the 'New Author' Finalist in
the 2020 Lesfic Bard Awards, celebrating
excellence in writing."
- Lesfic Bard Awards

"Emma Wallis did an excellent job in adding
dramatic suspense in This is Not a Love Story."
- Stephanie, Readers Favorite

"Skilful character development, especially
showing Scarlet's transition into adulthood."

"A thoughtful and interesting story, with a very

THIS IS NOT A LOVE STORY

EMMA WALLIS

ISBN: 9798695261165

Cover image sourced from www.freepik.com

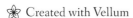 Created with Vellum

Foreword

Thank you, reader, for giving me the opportunity to tell you this story.

This is my debut novel and I'm delighted to say that it placed as the finalist in it's category of 'New Author' in the Lesfic Bard Awards.

This book features British Sign Language (BSL). If you'd like to learn more about BSL, or see what the signs look like then I recommend visiting:

www.britishsignlanguage.com

www.british-sign.co.uk

Or you can download the app that Scarlet uses in the book:

www.signBSL.com

Chapter One

Scarlet stood in the bay window and wiped the sill with a microfibre duster. Her hands sweated in a Pavlovian response to looking out of the window. She pushed her thumbnail into the rubber seal, just like she'd done so many times as a child. The rubber was brittle now, and some of it came away under her short nail.

Twelve years earlier, a much younger Scarlet sat on the sill in the same bay window, small sweaty palms pressed up against the glass as she stared out onto the driveway. Her stepdad Brian pushed a large Dalesbury University duffle bag into the boot of his car. The bag sagged open and one of his white work shirts spilled out. After he slammed the boot closed, one arm hung down over the bumper.

The driveway was wet from the earlier rain. As Brian drove away, the tyres splashed up muddy water onto the white sleeve waving behind the car.

Scarlet could hear her mother Marie in the kitchen. Glass bottles clattered together and then there was the slosh of liquid into a glass. She was too little to understand her mother's drinking, but she knew to be a good girl and keep out of her way.

"Scarlet!" Marie called from the back of the house. Scarlet turned away from the window, her hands leaving damp prints on the glass. She pressed her thumbnail into the rubber seal until the nail bed went white, leaving a small crescent shape behind. She slid off the windowsill and trailed toward the kitchen and the sound of her mother's voice.

"I've finished cleaning the lounge," an adult Scarlet called to her mother. Marie wandered around the doorway with a glass of wine in her hand. Glancing at the clock, Scarlet noted silently that it was only just an acceptable time of day to be drinking.

"Remember, mum, Maggie from Spotless Cleaning is going to come for two hours each Monday. She'll do a general clean and change the bedding in your room. You can leave her a note if you want her to do anything different."

Marie rolled her eyes at her daughter. Her hands moved as she spoke, and the wine was in real danger of spilling out of her glass. "Darling, I don't know why you're so worried. I am the adult here, am I not? You're such a mother hen."

Scarlet huffed and tried to move past her mother into the hallway. She had to squeeze against the frame to get through without knocking the glass of wine that was being pointed at her.

When she got to the kitchen, she flung the duster into the washing machine and slumped into a chair at the table. She ran her hands through her shoulder-length hair in frustration. The truth was, she worried about her mother. Marie was between husbands again, and she was a serial monogamist and didn't function well when not in a relationship. The wine and spirits were back, and the house would soon be a tip without Scarlet there to keep on top of it.

It was the worst possible time for Scarlet to be heading off to university. She decided it was necessary to organise for a cleaner to come in once a week, and she had booked for a grocery delivery at the same time every Friday evening.

She would not let her mum ruin this for her. She turned nineteen last week, and tomorrow she would move an hour away, into a student house next to the university campus.

The next morning Scarlet finished putting the last few smaller items into her bag. The night before, she packed her car with all the bigger stuff: A vacuum-packed duvet and pillows; a suitcase full of her clothes; a TV monitor that would double up as a larger screen for her iPad.

Looking around her bedroom one last time, Scarlet threw her bag over her shoulder, sure she had everything. Her plan was to not come home until Reading Week at October half-term.

Marie was sitting at the kitchen table when Scarlet came downstairs. She was clutching a glass of orange juice a little too closely to her chest. "Ready to go, mum?"

"Oh, no, darling. I don't think you want me to come. You get off and start your new life without your mother. Enjoy your independence." There was a spiteful tone to Marie's voice that made Scarlet's heart sink. All along the plan had been for her mother to drive down with her, help her get settled, then they would go out for lunch before Marie got the train home.

"Please, mum, we were going to have a nice last day together—"

"Well, I don't really see the point darling, it's a long way to go just for lunch."

"But it's not *just lunch* mum, it's a chance for us to spend time together because I'm moving away."

"Oh, are you, darling? I never would have guessed." Marie's spite was out in full force now. Scarlet turned her face away from her mother as she felt tears sting the corners of her eyes.

"Okay, bye then." She said in a small voice, bending down to kiss her mother's cheek. She breathed in, expecting to inhale the familiar scent of Chanel No. 5, but instead, she caught the smell of alcohol mixed in with the orange juice.

Standing up sharply, she backed away, nearly tripping as her foot caught the other chair. She turned and hurried out to her car.

Marie stood in the bay window, the nearly empty glass of vodka-orange clutched in her hand. She fingered the gouged out bits of the rubber seal, then pressed her hand against the window.

Her daughter's watery eyes met hers in the wing mirror of the car for a moment before Scarlet started the car and turned onto the road.

Once the little Ford Fiesta was out of sight, Marie poured herself another drink. She sat at the kitchen table and browsed her favourite shopping websites on her laptop. Lost in the world of online shopping, she jumped when the post dropped onto the doormat.

She staggered slightly getting up to retrieve the post, pressing her fingers into her temple to ward off a headache. She had to lean heavily on the wall as she bent to pick up the letters. Most of them looked like bills, and they went straight into a designated drawer of the sideboard. She could feel a hard rectangle inside the last envelope, and she took it back to the table and quickly tore it open.

Smiling, Marie pulled the new credit card off of the paper. She flicked the laptop screen back to the shopping cart page and used the new card to pay for the Michael Kors handbag she had saved. A satisfying ping announced the payment had been accepted. She relaxed at the sound, feeling the anxious energy drain from her limbs.

Her phone rang, and she looked at the screen, seeing the tiny digital photo of her friend Suzanne. She put her on speakerphone as she made herself a fresh vodka-orange. She was feeling good, the pleasure of making the purchase coursing through her.

"Suzanne, darling. Do you want to meet for lunch?"

Her friend's thin voice came through the phone, "I would love to, Marie. How about Ramsey's?"

"Oh no darling, let's go to the golf club restaurant. There'll be much more choice there. I am on the lookout for an eligible bachelor after all."

Chapter Two

Scarlet parked up outside her student house-share at 11am. She collected the keys from the letting agent the previous week when she had driven over to Dalesbury to sign the tenancy agreement.

Over the last month, she had been chatting back and forth with her three housemates. None of them had met before. They all applied to the agent separately via the university's accommodation service, but they seemed to get on well. They knew the basics about each other, but only time and close quarters would either cement their friendship or have them desperately seeking a new house-share for next year. Scarlet hoped for the former rather than the latter.

Their new home was a tall, thin townhouse with four bedrooms over the top two floors. The ground floor had a large kitchen-diner and communal living room.

Jessica flung open the door as Scarlet raised her key towards the lock. She was a bubbly older girl who had taken a gap year before uni to travel across Australia. Her long blonde hair was sun-bleached, and she wore a T-shirt with a print of a camper van on it. On her wrists she wore a collection of festival bracelets and bangles, which jangled as she moved.

She insisted Scarlet leave her bags in the car and come into the kitchen for a cup of tea straight away. *Jessica is... enthusiastic! It must have been lonely for her in the house by herself, just waiting for the rest of us to arrive.*

The house was sunny, and the kitchen had doors that led out onto a small patio. Jessica had opened the doors to let the fresh autumn air inside.

As she sat and enjoyed the sweet cup of tea, Scarlet felt herself relax a bit and let out an involuntary sigh.

"Are you ok?" Jessica asked. "You seem a bit down. Not excited to be starting uni?"

Scarlet smiled wanly at her new housemate. Jessica was so friendly and Scarlet didn't want to start their friendship off with a lie. "It's just my mum. I thought she was going to come with me today, but we must've crossed wires because she turned out to be busy this morning."

Conveniently, she left out that her mother waited until this morning to choose not to come. She was sure it was her fault anyway. Her mother relied on her. If only she could be a better daughter, then Marie would love her more and wouldn't need to lash out when Scarlet did something wrong.

Jessica gave her a kind smile and hopped up from her chair. Scarlet wasn't sure what Jessica was doing at first, but then she climbed up onto the worktop and reached for the top shelf of the cupboard. "This calls for the good chocolate biscuits," Jessica said with a grin as she passed down the old-fashioned, hinged biscuit tin.

They were still sitting at the kitchen table, drinking their tea and eating the biscuits when a knock sounded at the front door.

"Oh," Jessica clapped her hands. "That must be another one of our housemates." Smiling widely, she skipped down the hallway. Scarlet reached for another chocolate biscuit and then followed Jessica.

The girl on the steps was short, with a mop of curly black hair and fashionable big black-rimmed glasses. She wore linen trousers and a strappy top, a thin pashmina looped around her neck.

"Hi, I'm Kemsiyet but everyone calls me Kemi; well, except my old Egyptian grandparents."

Jessica hugged Kemi in the doorway, not even letting her get inside before she was engulfed in the taller girl's arms. "Salam 'alaykum Kemi. I'm Jessica, and this is Scarlet. Do you want tea? We were just having tea and biscuits."

"Oooo what sort of biscuits?" Kemi stepped into the

hallway, toed out of her shoes and followed the others back towards the kitchen.

Later that afternoon, the three new roommates were sitting on the patio. Finished with the chore of unpacking their bags, they now made the most of the early autumn sun. Jessica and Kemi's rooms were on the middle floor of the house, sharing a bathroom. Scarlet's room was on the top floor, she would be sharing a bathroom with Lily, who was yet to arrive.

The girls chatted and got to know each other. They seemed nice, and Scarlet began to relax in her new home. The others hadn't been dropped off by their parents. Perhaps her mother had been right. *Of course she'd been right. Marie always was.*

Later that night, Scarlet tossed and turned in bed, but sleep wouldn't come. For the hundredth time, she turned over and buried her face in the pillow. The bedding smelled new; it had a faint, plasticity odour that made her nose itch. Huffing, she flipped back over to stare up at the ceiling. She grabbed her phone from the bedside table and looked at the screen. It cast her face in a blue-tinged glow as she read the time: 1:04.

She turned off the screen and pressed the edge of the phone against her forehead. Closing her eyes, she dumped it back onto the table. *You're an independent woman now, Scarlet, so for God's sake, go to sleep!*

There was light coming in around the sides of the curtains. The streetlights were brighter here than at home. She made a disgusted noise at herself and pulled the duvet over her head. There was no reason to be homesick. She was starting her exciting new life, with exciting new people, in a place that was all the more exciting because her mother wasn't there. It should feel like bliss.

The sound of a car braking sharply pulled her out of her thoughts. Several car doors opened and closed with a slam. The chatter of several people talking over each other rose up to her bedroom window. She was too far away to hear what they were saying, but it sounded like a family exchanging friendly banter with each other.

It was enough of a distraction to bring her out of the thoughts of her mother, and Scarlet finally drifted off to sleep.

Chapter Three

The sun breaking through her new curtains woke Scarlet the next morning. She pulled a hoodie over her pyjama top and wandered downstairs looking for breakfast. The girls brought some basics with them like cereal and milk, but they were going to do an online shop together today.

The house was quiet as she made herself a bowl of her favourite cereal and took it outside to sit on the patio. The air was a bit crisper this morning, but the sky was blue. It promised to warm up as the day went on. A small bird landed on the fence, and Scarlet watched it as she ate. Another one soon joined the first and they twittered to each other and puffed their feathers.

"Hello?" An unfamiliar voice caught Scarlet off guard with her spoon halfway to her mouth. She dropped the spoon into the bowl with a clatter and splashed milk onto her hand. The two birds flew away, tweeting angrily. Turning back towards the open patio doors, Scarlet saw a stranger in the kitchen.

The stranger was around her age, wearing pyjamas. She had big fluffy socks on her feet and her brown hair was tousled from sleep. She was clearly not a burglar.

Scarlet stared at her open-mouthed for several beats before she found her voice and stammered, "Um, hi. Can I help you?"

The girl walked toward her and shielded her eyes with her hand as she stepped out through the doors. She took in the surprised look on Scarlet's face and dropped down into the other garden chair.

"I'm Lil. Sorry, you didn't know I was here, did you? We got in so late last night, it was after 1:00, and we tried to be quiet when we let ourselves in. Are you Scarlet? I think we're going to be floormates." Lil, Lily, spoke in a quick voice, like she had loads to say and a finite time to say it in. She finished speaking with a massive grin.

Scarlet nodded her head, "Yep, that's me. And no, I didn't know you'd arrived last night. Uh, you said 'we', who's 'we'?"

"Oh right. My mum and dad dropped me off. It was too late for them to go to a hotel so they stayed in my room for the night, and I slept on the sofa."

Scarlet felt her throat tighten at the reminder she had expected her own mother to drop her off yesterday.

She flashed back to Marie's slightly drooping head as she kissed her goodbye at their kitchen table, the sharp smell of Marie's drink in her nostrils.

As quickly as the image came, it disappeared and Scarlet tried to refocus on Lily's kind face.

"I was just going to put the kettle on," Lily said. "Do you want a drink?"

Scarlet followed her into the kitchen and washed up her bowl while the other girl slid around on the tiles in her socks, opening and closing different cupboards, looking for the fixings for tea and coffee. She set everything out on the table and as Scarlet was putting her now dried bowl back in the cupboard, Jessica and Kemi came into the room. They all greeted the new arrival, and Lily grabbed extra mugs for them.

It wasn't long before they all heard footsteps making their way down the stairs from the top floor, and then Lily's parents stood in the doorway of the kitchen.

"We're sorry, girls," Lily's dad wrapped his arm around his wife's waist as he spoke. "We didn't mean to intrude on you in your new home."

They were met with a chorus of "It's fine" and "anytime" from the girls.

Amazing. Scarlet never heard a parent apologise to their child before. It was a completely foreign concept to her. Her mother never apologised for anything. She would rather blame anyone but herself, including her daughter. It was something so simple, but hearing such a heartfelt apology from a concerned parent made Scarlet's chest ache.

Lily's parents pulled up chairs at the table and joined the girls for breakfast. They matched Scarlet's first impressions of Lily: fun and kind.

The next few days were a whirlwind of getting to know each other and settling into the house. They crowded around the kitchen table at mealtimes, and in the evenings they piled into the living room to watch films together. Jessica was doing a degree in Modern Languages, Kemi was doing Art and Design, Lily was at the medical school, training to be a midwife, and Scarlet's degree was Developmental Psychology.

They all had such different interests and personalities, but that didn't stop them becoming friends.

Living with three other girls came with its own teething problems. Sometimes, Kemi got annoyed when someone used up her oat milk, and Jessica kept forgetting to lock the bathroom door. Scarlet accidentally used Lily's toothbrush because she couldn't remember hers was the blue one. There had been no major arguments, though. All the bedrooms were the same size, so there was no jealousy over who had which room. They took it in turns to pick what to watch on movie night, but they had to veto Jessica's beloved foreign horror films.

Their first week at the university, Induction Week, wasn't going to start for another few days so they explored the area surrounding the house, and went shopping for things they agreed the house needed.

———

The day had been unusually cool for mid-September, and Scarlet put on a big woolly jumper and socks by late afternoon to ward off the chill. The girls sat on the patio with the fire pit lit between them, eating cheese on toast. They laughed as they played a word association game, and Lily produced a bag of marshmallows.

In her room that night, Scarlet was getting ready for bed when she heard her text alert. A glance at the lit-up notification screen showed a message from her mother.

She hadn't heard from Marie since that horrible morning last week. The morning where Marie had cast her off into the world.

Her heart leapt for a moment. She had hope for that idyllic mother-daughter relationship that had always been just out of their grasp. She opened the text.

U shud make it a priority 2 join the most expensive gym u can find. U won't find urself a rich wife at sum cheap student place. Remember the Freshers 15, u don't want to gain that weight do u? xoxo

Marie was still decidedly true to form. Now she was

just doing it from an hour away, still pushing her own priorities onto her daughter. Scarlet blew a frustrated stream of air out her nose. *No danger of a move from our mother/daughter status quo then, mum?*

She needed a few minutes to calm down before replying, so she popped across the landing to the bathroom and completed her bedtime routine. Once she was back in her room, she climbed into bed and shot off a quick message.

It's too expensive mum x

Marie's reply came back almost instantly.

U've got 2 spend money 2 make money xoxo

Scarlet tossed her phone onto the bed in exasperation. *Mum doesn't see things the way other people do. She sashays through life getting what she wants with the help of some rather questionable morals. Her idea of looking after herself involves finding a wealthy spouse to pay for her lifestyle.*

Chapter Four

"**D**ance Monkey! Can you turn this song up, babes?!" Lily squealed. Scarlet flicked the volume up from five to eight, a nice round number. They danced in their seats as they sang along with Tones and I. "Just like a monkey I've been dancing my whole life. But you just beg to see me dance just one more time."

They were driving home from a Sunday afternoon shopping trip. As Scarlet turned onto their road, they saw their housemates weaving down the pavement, carrying something between them like a pair of builders would carry a ladder.

"What on *earth* is that?!" Lily called out the window to Jessica and Kemi as Scarlet scrambled to turn the radio down at the same time as she slowed the car to a crawl next to them.

Kemi beamed. "I found the most beautiful rug for the living room. Some guys were doing a house clearance in the road behind ours, and they were about to throw it in the skip! I think it might be an authentic Turkish carpet. I had to save it!"

Scarlet frowned as she looked between the girls and the hill they were about to climb towards their house. Ten minutes later they managed to push the rolled-up rug onto the roof of her car. It bent over the front and one end rested on the bonnet. With the other three housemates walking beside to tell her if it started to slip off, Scarlet drove slowly up the hill. The engine revved more than normal as she rode the clutch to ensure they didn't roll backwards.

They were near their house when two things happened at the same time. The massive rug did indeed start to slide off the front of the car when the hill levelled out, and a dog started barking.

Scarlet braked, which caused the rug to slide all the way off.

The girls all looked around for the sound of barking, wondering whether a neighbour's dog had escaped from its garden.

Through a gap between two parked cars, they spotted the dog on the pavement. It was a wire-haired terrier wearing a purple coat. It barked, then turned in a tight circle, then barked again. An owner that they couldn't see behind a car held it on a loose lead.

Jessica was the nearest to the barking dog, so she went to investigate while the others moved the rug out of the road.

That evening the four friends sat on their new rug in front of the TV, an extra-large pizza box open on the coffee table. Tomorrow was going to be the first day of their induction week, or Freshers' Week as the students called it.

They would have introduction talks from their heads of faculty, induction sessions for the library and computer suites, and tours of different parts of the campus. The week would officially end with the Freshers' Fair, a chance for all the First Year students to find out about the social clubs and sports teams at the university. Unofficially there was a pub-crawl around the town for the new students. It was a rite of passage not to be missed, and the girls looked forward to it.

They sat with their backs against the sofas, the flickering light from the film bathing their faces. Scarlet felt her phone buzz in her pocket, and she pulled it out to look at the screen.

Mother.

She excused herself and waited until she was in the hallway before swiping to accept the call, mentally crossing her fingers Marie would be in a good mood. "Hi mum—"

Her hope was dashed as Marie launched into a rant as soon as Scarlet answered the phone. "That Maggie woman, the cleaner, moved the kettle. Supposedly to clean under it and didn't put it back in the right place. Now I can't find my favourite jacket. First, I thought the cleaner stole it, but that's ridiculous. She's a fat woman who would never fit in my size 8 linen blazer. No stretch in linen, you see, darling. The Ocado delivery driver dared to knock ten minutes early. How dare he disturb me? And to top it all off they substituted a two-pinter of milk for a four-pinter, how do they think I'm going to have room for that in my fridge?!"

Scarlet bit back a retort that she was sure her mother could fit the milk if she didn't have so many bottles of wine vying for space in the fridge.

"Mum you can't say things like that about people, Maggie isn't fat. You can't just go around making sizeist comments."

"Oh, come off it darling, you and your psychology."

"Fat-shaming is real, mum," Scarlet shook her head. Her mum was terrible for saying things about other people's looks or the clothes they wore. Anyone thinner than Marie was "anorexic" and anyone bigger was "too fat to wear that. What does she think she looks like?"

"Darling, can you just phone the cleaners and ask them to tell that woman to find my jacket?"

"Seriously, mum… She's not a psychic. How is Maggie supposed to know where you left your coat? It's probably in your car." Scarlet pinched the bridge of her nose. She could feel a headache coming on. It had been less than a week since she'd spoken to her mother, but she had started to detox from her. She made a mental note to get Maggie an extra big box of chocolates for Christmas for putting up with Marie.

Marie hung up with her daughter five minutes later with insincere well- wishes for the first day of term. *It's bad enough Scarlet moved away from me, but to leave me to fend for myself is the worst sin a daughter could commit. I need to find a new husband. Yes, I'll visit the golf club tomorrow.*

As she went to close the curtains at the front of the house, she glanced out of the window at her car. There on the parcel shelf was the unmistakable shape of her linen jacket.

Chapter Five

Monday turned out to be a beautiful September day. The early morning was crisp, with the promise of sun. Scarlet quickly got into a routine of eating her breakfast on the patio, and she would be sad when the weather turned cold and forced her indoors.

Today was the first day of Freshers' Week, and all four girls were going in together for the meet and greet sessions with their personal tutors. Each faculty was housed in their own building on campus, along with the communal buildings, the library, the admin building, the Student's Union and a sports centre.

Once they were all ready for the day, they piled into Scarlet's car. On the drive to campus, they buzzed with excitement, and the car filled with chatter as they talked about what they would each be doing. Normally they would walk to their lectures and seminars, but they took the car today because University Press Books would be in the Student Union with a pop-up bookshop where they could buy the most up-to-date textbooks for their courses. They each needed several heavy books, and they wanted to drop them off in the car instead of carrying them around all day.

The university car park was already packed at 9:30, so it took Scarlet a while to find an empty spot at the back.

"I'm so glad our house is close enough to walk here," Kemi said as she slung her giant shoulder bag over her arm, more fashion accessory than practical. "Can you imagine what a nightmare it would be to park here every single day?" The others all made various sounds of agreement as they unfolded themselves from the small car.

"Okay, meet back here with your books at midday, girls," Scarlet said as she consulted the emailed timetable on her phone.

"Great, we can get some lunch before our computer clinic at two o'clock," Jessica said before she smiled and dashed off toward the languages building.

Bored, Marie scrolled through the contacts in her phone, looking for someone to talk to. *Is it today that Suzanne's taking her mother to a hospital appointment? Her phone's probably turned off.*

What about Caroline? No. She didn't need to hear anymore of her cousin's hippy nonsense if she could avoid it.

She surveyed her options. Her finger hovered over the name Greg. He was a dentist she met a few weeks ago. His divorce was nearly finalised, but he had a couple of kids younger than Scarlet. She moved on. *What about Mark, the coach driver? He could get me some cheap holidays, if I could bear to sit on a coach with fifty pensioners. But his beer belly is so... distasteful. I couldn't have* that.

Scarlet? Well, it is her first day at uni, but it's only Freshers' Week. She won't really be busy, will she? It's only a stupid Mickey Mouse degree anyway. Marie told her daughter to choose business or law, so Scarlet could look after her mother properly.

She hit the call button.

Mum. Scarlet groaned when she looked at her phone screen. She debated not answering for a second, but then decided it would just be worse when she did eventually talk to her. Standing outside the seminar room, she glanced at the time. She'd arrived a bit early for the meet and greet session with her personal tutor, so she had time for a quick chat. She rested her back against the wall and swiped the screen to answer. "Hello, mum."

"Scarlet darling. How are you? What are you doing?"

"Well, I'm just waiting—"

Marie cut her off. "Fantastic, darling. I've just come back from the hairdressers. I didn't want anything too drastic, but I let the young man put some extra texturing in at the back. I'll send you a photo later."

Scarlet let her mother talk at her on the other end of the phone while her mind drifted to her day. She looked forward to meeting the other people in her tutor group. She wondered what her tutor would be like. The information pack the Psychology department sent out said his name was Dr Carl Baker, and he would be her primary point of contact for the next three years.

A few other people started to arrive, most carrying takeaway coffee cups. They slipped into the seminar rooms on either side of the corridor. Scarlet glanced at the time, and looked jealously at the other students' caffeine fix. "Mum, I think I might just go grab a cup of coffee before my session starts."

"Oh darling, do you think that's wise? You don't want to get coffee stains on your teeth, do you? If you must drink it, be sure to use a straw like I taught you to protect your teeth. God knows I spent enough money on orthodontist appointments for you."

Marie carried on talking, but it just became a drone

in Scarlet's ear. A tall woman with short dark hair walked down the corridor towards her. She wore dark jeans and a white dress shirt with the sleeves rolled up to the elbows. It did a nice job of exposing the bottom half of what must be a full sleeve tattoo on one arm. She wasn't a student — she was older and walked with the confidence of someone who knew where they were going. A lanyard with a staff ID swayed around her neck in confirmation.

She smiled at Scarlet as she got close to her. She almost walked past, but then stopped and handed Scarlet the full coffee she was carrying. "You've got Dr Baker? Here, you'll need this more than me."

She winked and turned into the door across the corridor.

Scarlet stared after her, a surprised smile plastered onto her face. "Sorry, mum, I didn't catch that. I've just met the most stunning woman I've ever seen. And she gave me a coffee — her coffee — by the looks of things."

"Well, be sure to sit next to her in class; perhaps you can get to know her. You might even get laid before the week is out. God knows you could do with something to relax you a bit. You're always so uptight, darling."

"She's not in my class, mum. I think she's a lecturer."

"Oh, *really*, Scarlet." Here it was, Marie's famous about-turn. "What kind of lesbian cliché do you think you are? Don't get involved. I mean, student/teacher romances are so out of fashion these days."

Marie huffed and hung up.

Scarlet stared at the blank phone for a full minute before sliding it back into her pocket. Holding the cardboard cup to her chest, she grabbed her bag and went to find a seat in her classroom.

Her mystery coffee-giver had been right, she did indeed need that caffeine. Dr Carl Baker was an older gentleman who wore his trousers pulled up so high that he could, and did, tuck his tie into them. He spoke in a very soft voice. She wasn't the only student yawning before the session was over.

There were twelve of them in the tutor group, divided into three study groups. Scarlet's group included a girl called Rebecca, and two boys named Stephen and Etienne. They were encouraged to meet up twice a week for group study sessions, and they would also work on a presentation together in one of their seminars.

Stephen was older, a mature student, he was returning to education after fifteen years working in a supermarket. Scarlet could hear her mother's voice in her head, "What does he think he's doing? Got a high opinion of himself, hasn't he?"

She could imagine what Marie would say about Etienne, "He should've stayed in his own country." And she would say it in such a way that it wouldn't be clear whether she meant because he was black or French.

Not even Rebecca would get away unscathed, "She would be so *pretty* if she used a bit of make-up."

Shaking off her mother's opinions, Scarlet decided not to pass any judgement on them until she got to know them better — a good first step in removing herself from Marie's mindset.

Chapter Six

On Tuesday it was raining. Not just a drizzle, but a full-on shower that made people think twice about going outside. Marie hated the rain for many reasons, but today her main gripe was that it would play havoc with her hair. *It's like the clouds know I had my hair done yesterday and are punishing me!*

She planned to play a round of golf with Greg The Dentist today. Vainly, she fluffed her hair. *Perhaps I could interest him in a game of squash instead?* She pulled her phone out to call him and saw Scarlet had changed her profile picture. She clicked on the tiny photo to see a bigger version. In the selfie, Scarlet grinned, holding a cardboard cup with someone else's name scrolled on its side.

Rhys.

Marie rolled her eyes. It hadn't taken her daughter long to drift off course.

Oh well, let her have her dalliances.

Her mother saw it as her job to guide her wayward child back to the matter at hand — networking in the right circles and making valuable connections. Ultimately, she intended for Scarlet to marry rich, just like Marie had been trying to do her entire life.

Thinking about Scarlet and her complete disregard for doing what was best for them made Marie feel anxious. Her skin prickled in a way that would only settle with alcohol or the thrill of a big splurge at the shops. Pouring her first drink of the day, she mentally flipped through the credit cards in her purse, trying to remember which weren't already maxed out to their limit. Rain wouldn't stop her from getting her fix. She could brave the umbrella-filled pavements if it meant getting to her favourite high-end shops. If worse came to worst, there was always online shopping. It didn't give her quite the same release of endorphins, but it would do.

When she opened the curtains that morning, Scarlet was sad to see the rain. She liked Autumn with its crisp air and the brown and red leaves which crunched underfoot. But she had learned to tread carefully on the wet pavements when the leaves turned to mush.

She had her induction for the library today. They had been in the library building yesterday for their computer clinic, where they were given the email addresses and passwords they would use to log on to the university network. The computer rooms were in the basement, and one large room held fifty computers and a bank of printers. Then there were several smaller rooms which held twenty computers each. These would normally be booked for computer-related classes. Her course didn't have many of those, but she would have to do a research project including quantifiable data processing in her second year.

The main computer room was open from 6 am to midnight for students who wanted to study on campus around their lectures and seminars. It was staffed by final-year students in red polo shirts. The library itself opened at 8am and closed at 8 pm, and was staffed by a mixture of librarians and student helpers.

The windows of the library were fogged up by everyone's wet clothes when Scarlet arrived with Jessica, her induction time-slot buddy. "It seems like everyone's ducked inside to escape the rain," Jessica said, trying not to let her coat drip onto the floor, "My induction sheet says 'meet at the enquiry desk', is that on the main floor?"

"I think so." Scarlet looked around. "This is the main floor, right?"

When they pushed through the entrance barrier from the lobby into the library, Jessica's face brightened, and she waved to someone over Scarlet's shoulder. "I see someone who can direct us!"

Scarlet turned to see one of the librarians waving back. Unlike the student helpers, who wore blue polo shirts, the librarians wore their own clothes with blue lanyards around their necks. The woman came around the circulation desk to greet Jessica, and Scarlet was surprised to see the terrier in the purple coat walking next to her. As they got closer, she could see the coat said "Don't Distract Me, I'm Working." When the librarian stopped, the dog stopped and sat next to her.

"Scarlet, this is Amy, I met her when we were trying to get Kemi's rug home." Jessica spoke to Scarlet but faced Amy, and as she spoke she used her hands in fluid movements that Scarlet recognised as sign language.

"Hello, Scarlet." Amy had a slight inflection to her voice, and Scarlet assumed this came from learning to speak by watching other people's lip and tongue movements rather than by sound. As she spoke she gave a brief wave and then touched her little fingers together like she was giving herself a pinky promise. A feeling of panic crept unbidden into Scarlet's chest.

"I'm sorry, I don't know any sign language," She

blurted, embarrassed that she didn't know how to communicate with this smiling lady.

"That's ok; I lip read. Just be sure to face me." Amy tapped the badge pinned to her lanyard, which had a picture of a hand cupping an ear and the words "Speak Clearly and Face Me" printed on it.

"Of course. I can do that," Scarlet said with relief. "Jessica, perhaps you could teach me some signs?"

Scarlet watched, captivated by the way Amy and Jessica communicated with their hands and facial expressions. She felt like she was missing out on something important but not like she was being excluded. On the contrary, the others kept up the verbal part of the conversation so she could follow what they were saying.

Ashamed, she twisted the strap of her bag.

She realised without Jessica's knowledge she would have just said hello to Amy and then awkwardly excused herself, not knowing how to have a conversation with someone different from herself. As they chatted she relaxed into the conversation. Jessica asked Amy how long she'd had her hearing dog.

"She's adorable." Jessica motioned to the little dog and touched two fingers to her forehead. "What's her name?"

"This is Peggy. She's a Lakeland Terrier." On hearing her name, Peggy popped her head up. Big brown eyes looked eagerly up at her mistress, but Amy made a subtle gesture, and she laid down again.

"She's very well behaved. What else is she trained to do?" Jessica asked.

"She alerts me to sounds like the fire alarm, the phone, doorbell, or someone calling my name."

"I'm sorry." Scarlet blushed before she asked what she was sure was a stupid question. "I'm sure this is a really ignorant question, but why does she need to tell you the phone is ringing?"

She felt so embarrassed and unworldly. Her mother was more likely to pull her away from anyone who wasn't just like them. Marie had always been obsessed with surrounding herself with, as she would say, "the best people." As a child, Scarlet wasn't allowed to play with the children who lived next door because their dad was Jamaican. Looking back now, Scarlet recognised it for what it was: smallmindedness, bordering on racism. Even then, when she didn't have the words to express how she felt, it made her feel uneasy. Unfortunately, her mother was her only point of reference for social cues. Marie sculpted her daughter as an effigy of her own beliefs. *I can just imagine what mum would say about Amy.*

"Well, I used to use a textphone system, but that was so slow. Now I mostly use video calls like FaceTime. I feel so lucky to be living in a time when we have so many communication technologies. Not long ago, my deafness would have completely isolated me." She patted her pocket in the universal action of looking for her phone, and said, "When I use my mobile I can feel the vibration alert if it's here in my pocket — or if I'm wearing my smartwatch — but if I leave it in my coat, or on the table, Peggy will come and tell me it's ringing. At work there's normally someone else to answer the phone, but I have video conferencing on the computer so faculty members can talk to me about research enquiries."

"Wow, I never would have thought about what a difference something like FaceTime could make to someone's life. That's wild."

"That's right. There are so many things we use every day that were originally invented as solutions for people with disabilities. Did you know the first type-writer — the precursor to the modern keyboard — was invented in the early 1800s for an Italian Countess who was blind? It was so she could write private letters without having to dictate them to another person. Also, audiobooks were first invented for soldiers who lost their vision because of mustard gas attacks in World War I."

"That's amazing!" Scarlet said. Amy's passion for the topic was evident as she spoke. *I wish I could find something I was that passionate about.*

After the tour of the library, Scarlet and Jessica waited in line to collect their library cards. The tour showed them which subjects were housed on which floor of the building, and how to use the self-service kiosks to issue and discharge their books.

"I didn't know you knew sign language," Scarlet said as they waited. "I knew you were studying modern languages, but I figured that would just be things like French and Spanish."

"Oh yeah, actually BSL was the first new language I learnt. My aunt is deaf, and I began learning to sign very young. I just have a knack for learning languages, and I love travelling. My parents took me all over the place when I was little. They even took me out of school for a year, and we drove across Europe in a converted bus."

"That sounds amazing, Jessica!"

"It was. I feel very lucky. I've always been able to immerse myself in whichever language I was learning."

"I would love to learn sign language. I learnt a bit of Makaton at school, but I know it's not the same as BSL."

"I can definitely teach you some signs. BSL has its own grammar structure, but you can start off with Sign-Assisted English and then work on the BSL grammar. Actually, I think I saw a poster in the Languages Building for a BSL evening class; I can grab you the details?"

"That would be great. Just take a photo of the poster and text it to me?"

"Absolutely."

Chapter Seven

Lectures started on Thursday for Scarlet. The first one was Introduction to Psychology and the faculty head Dr Hunter would be taking the lecture. She was excited to get an overview of the course and find out what modules they would do this term. It was also going to be her first time in the main lecture theatre, with its tiered seating and big projection screen. She felt like this was the real beginning of her university life.

The lecture was due to start at ten o'clock that morning. The rain stopped just after breakfast, and Scarlet left herself plenty of time to walk from her student house to the psychology building. She was rounding the corner, the entrance in sight, when the sky decided she needed a second shower of the day. She made a run for the protection of the doorway, but by the time she got inside, her hair and clothes were already soaked.

"Just great," Scarlet muttered under her breath as she pulled her wet top away from her skin. Her new jeans stuck to her thighs, and she knew they hadn't been through the wash enough yet; her legs were bound to be stained blue underneath the denim.

She ducked into the loo to dance around in front of the hand dryer until it was time for the lecture to begin.

"Are you alright?"

Scarlet whipped round at the voice close behind her. The hand dryer was loud and powerful, so she hadn't been aware anyone else had come into the toilets.

Her coffee benefactor stood there, a look of concern on her handsome face. Scarlet stared at her dumbly, her T-shirt pinched between her fingers to pull it away from her chest. Tall, Dark, and Generous glanced down at the damp fabric and cocked an eyebrow.

Scarlet was glad she could attribute the heat in her cheeks to the hot air from the dryer. Letting the fabric fall back against her chest, she was glad she'd worn a padded bra today. She was already embarrassed enough; she didn't need to be giving this woman an eyeful of her pebbled nipples either.

"Are you alright?" She asked again, making Scarlet realise she'd been silent for too long.

"I'm fine, really. I thought the rain had stopped and got caught out. It was my own fault. I should have checked my weather app before I left this morning. I need to keep an umbrella in my bag—" Scarlet pulled herself up short when she realised she'd gone from silence to rambling in 0.3 seconds.

"I think that's the last of the rain for today, but an umbrella sounds like a good idea." The woman, Rhys, said. She turned with a smile, "I'll catch you later, coffee girl."

Later, as it turned out, was much sooner than Scarlet expected. The wet T-shirt incident meant she was left to sneak into the back of the lecture theatre after they shut the doors. She shuffled into the first available seat with her head down and her hand already digging in her bag for her iPad.

Her head popped up, and her eyes went wide at the familiar voice coming over the speakers. A look down at the podium confirmed that yes, indeed, Rhys stood there in front of Scarlet's cohort of psychology students. As she introduced herself she flicked on the projection screen and there it was, in massive letters on the first slide:

Introduction to Psychology
Dr Rhys Hunter

Scarlet groaned internally. Just her luck that the gorgeous woman she kept running into was the head of her course. Not just the head of her course—Dr Hunter was the faculty head for the whole Psychology department. Scarlet settled back into her seat and tried to concentrate on what Rhys was saying about this module, instead of being distracted by her smooth, sexy voice.

An hour later the other students were filing out of the lecture theatre while Scarlet scrolled back through the slides on her iPad, painfully aware of how few annotations she made on them. *Shit, how am I going to concentrate on her lectures? At least it'll be different faculty members giving lectures on their specialist subjects, so I won't completely screw up this whole module.*

She flipped the case closed and slid the iPad into her bag with a sigh.

"Hey Scarlet, do you want to come with us for a coffee, and we can pin down some days for study group?" Rebecca stood with Etienne in the aisle, playing with the end of her ponytail.

"You know what? That sounds great." Scarlet gave a small smile and looked around to see if Rhys was still at the podium. She had been toying with the ill-advised idea of making up an excuse to go talk to her coffee benefactor again. For the whole lecture she'd obsessed about the need to show Rhys she was more than just a tongue-tied, dumb girl. She had gone over the scene by the hand dryer over and over in her head, replaying what she could have said to make her sound funny or interesting, or even just capable of stringing together some intelligent words.

"If you're looking for Stephen he's gone on ahead to

grab us a table." Rebecca said, getting Scarlet's attention again. She snapped her focus back to the people standing in the aisle in front of her and mentally scolded herself for being so rude.

Fifteen minutes later the four Psychology students sat together at a table in the student union, a mug of coffee in front of each of them. Rebecca had pulled her own mug out of her bag and handed it over to the barista. Scarlet admired the confidence with which Rebecca owned the action, even though she was the only person who brought their own mug.

They got to know each other between sorting out a time and place to meet up for their first proper study group session. They decided to meet next week in a study pod in the library. Scarlet offered to go to the library on her way home and book the pod. Before they left the student union they set up a WhatsApp group so she could let them know the time.

The library was much busier than the last time Scarlet had been there. Several groups of students stood around on the ground floor at various stages of their inductions, another group lined up in front of the desk to get their new library cards. Today there were more student helpers. They buzzed about in their blue shirts putting out trolleys of what appeared to be new books. They reminded Scarlet of hummingbirds.

She joined the end of the queue for the enquiry desk and settled in to wait and pulled her phone out of her pocket, idly scrolling through Facebook to pass the time. She immediately noticed a post by Marie. She was at the golf club smiling and holding onto the arm of a grey-haired man who was holding a bag of golf clubs over his shoulder. The caption read: "Being taught a thing or two by a real man."

Blurgh.

Scarlett didn't know whether to roll her eyes or scoff in disgust. Her mother was up to her old tricks. This must be the man her mother planned to get her claws into next. She wondered how her mother could keep picking up new men at the golf club. Surely she needed a fresh hunting ground by now.

She found it baffling how easily Marie could pick up these men. There was certainly nothing wrong with her self-esteem. Scarlett wished she could have even a fraction of the self-confidence her mother had. She never entertained the idea that she'd have a problem getting a date with whichever man she set her sights on.

Scarlet hovered her finger over the picture to see the tags. Oh there it was: Greg The Dentist. She heard her mother talk about him on the phone with Suzanne. Was he separated or divorced? Did he have kids? It probably didn't matter to Marie.

It was just easier when Marie's new man came to the relationship on his own, with no children to complicate matters. It was also far better if he came to the relationship already divorced. It made things much less messy.

Scarlet looked at the picture and held down the "like" button until it showed her the different reactions. Not for the first time, she wished Facebook had an "eye rolling" reaction. She debated with herself for another minute and then clicked away. It was best not to react at all. If Marie mentioned the picture, she would pretend she hadn't seen it.

Scarlet got to the front of the queue and smiled to see Amy behind the desk.

"Hello, Scarlet. How can I help?" As she spoke Amy made a thumbs up with her right hand and placed it on top of her flat left palm, moving the sign from in front of herself toward Scarlet. Scarlet was touched that Amy remembered her name. She also remembered Scarlet expressed an interest in learning sign language.

She smiled at Amy, but it didn't really reach her eyes, caught up as she was still thinking about her mother. "Can I book a study pod for next week, please?"

"Of course you can, but what's wrong?" The genuine concern in Amy's face brought tears to Scarlet's eyes. She pressed her fingers to the bridge of her nose to keep the tears from falling.

"Oh, sweetie. Wait here while I get someone to cover the desk." Amy tugged Scarlet to the side and held up a finger to the person behind her in the queue in the universal signal for "wait a moment."

Before she knew it, a blue-shirted helper was getting the queue moving again, and Amy was leading her through to the librarians' office. They sat in low chairs, and Amy released Peggy with a hand signal. The small dog trotted off to a bowl in the corner of the room for a loud slurp of water before returning to curl up at Amy's feet.

The librarian reached forward as if to touch Scarlet's hand, but then retreated to a respectful distance. "Can you tell me what's wrong?"

A tear slid down Scarlet's cheek. Why was a practical stranger being so nice to her? She took the tissue that seemed to appear magically in Amy's hand and pressed it to her face. "It's nothing really... just my mum..."

Amy gently touched her knee and said, "I can't see what you're saying when you have your hand in front of your mouth."

Scarlet looked up into her kind eyes. She dried her face and put the tissue on her lap. "I'm sorry, Amy. I didn't think—"

"It's," She paused for a second, a slight frown creasing between her eyebrows, "fine, I understand you're not used to someone reading your lips. But listen, when you apologise for something like that convention dictates I tell you 'it's okay' or 'it's fine' when for me it actually isn't." She softened her words with a smile. "You'll do better in the future. Now, what were you saying?"

It felt strange to Scarlet to have someone give her their undivided attention. Amy looked at her and really saw her. She wasn't just looking in order to read her lips; she was looking like she really cared about what Scarlet had to say.

"I was just thinking about my mum."

When Scarlet finished crying, Amy made sure she would be able to get home safely. It hadn't started to get dark yet, and she reassured her new friend that her route home was short. As she walked along the pavement, she pressed her fingers to her temples. Despite the headache behind her eyes, she felt lighter than she had in a long time.

At home that evening, Scarlet thought back to the time she'd spent with Amy. Naturally, the other woman thought she was homesick when she mentioned her mum. She explained it wasn't exactly homesickness, but the overriding feeling her mum didn't care that her only child was no longer living at home. *She only cares that she doesn't have me as her very own live-in personal assistant anymore. She'd love a PA to boss around. Someone who could make sure all the important things get done, and wouldn't voice an opinion on her behaviour. She'd love that set up so much more than a daughter who tries to make her accountable for her actions.* It was true, in the short time Scarlet had been gone, her mother seemed thrilled to not be beholden to her teenage daughter anymore.

Amy can't even hear my voice, yet she listened to me with such empathy, I could see the compassion in her eyes. How is it that I feel so heard by someone who can't hear at all? Amy didn't need sound. The words Scarlet spoke were only a small element in the grand scheme of things. Amy didn't just read her lips, but read her facial expression and body language too. Scarlet couldn't help but tear up again. Sat in the library office with Amy, she just kept thinking over and over, *Why are you being so nice to me? What have I done to deserve your kindness?*

It was still so easy to allow Marie into her head, chipping away at her. *Do you really think you deserve kindness, Darling? It's sweet you think that, but what have you given them in return?*

Chapter Eight

On Friday there were no lectures or seminars. All the First Years had their schedules cleared for the Freshers' Fair.

All of the uni's clubs and societies wanted to attract new members, so they tried to outdo each other with banners, table decorations, and freebies. Even the most antisocial First Years went to the Freshers' Fair for the freebies.

Scarlet's headache wasn't really any better when she woke up that morning. She groaned and reached for the paracetamol in her bedside table drawer. Luckily, she still had a bottle of water beside her bed from the night before. She eyed it, hoping there was just enough left in the bottle to wash down the two tablets. She couldn't understand why, in this age of science and technology, the pharmacological industry hadn't yet invented tablets the size of a pinhead. The second tablet got stuck in her throat, and she had to rush over to the bathroom to get more water to wash it down. So much for a cheeky lie in to get rid of the headache.

She was up for the day now; there wasn't any chance of her getting back to sleep. As she came downstairs, she could hear Jessica knocking on Kemi's door, chanting, "Swag. Swag. Swag."

Scarlet rolled her eyes, *Jessica obviously has really high hopes for the freebies at the Freshers' Fair.* "Good morning, Jessica."

Jessica turned and smiled at Scarlett. "Good morning to you, too. How's the headache?"

Scarlett groaned and pressed her head against the wall in the hallway, looking at Jessica out of the corner of her eye.

"Oh dear, that bad, eh?" Jessica returned to knocking on Kemi's door, more softly this time out of respect for Scarlett's sore head.

Thank goodness, the rain's let up, Scarlet thought as the four housemates walked along the road to the campus. They could already see some gazebos set up on The Green for the overflow of the fair. The Fair originally fit in the sports centre in the middle of campus. Now, there were so many clubs, teams, and societies the centre was too small and the event spilt out.

Before they entered, Jessica huddled them together like a team of American football players. "Right girls, listen. We need to divide and conquer if we're going to get the best freebies. We don't need loads of pens and pencils. We need to concentrate on the good stuff. Kemi and I will take the outside stalls. Scarlet and Lil, you do a round of the stalls inside the sports hall. We'll text each other which clubs are giving away the best swag!"

"Isn't the point of the fair for us to see which clubs we might want to join?" Lily asked.

"Well, yeah, but let's get the important bit out of the way first. We can make a second pass later to visit any of the stalls for more information about what the clubs actually do. The Fair is on all day after all, but the freebies will run out soon." The other three girls just smiled and shook their heads at Jessica, then they reached the entrance and dived into the chaos that was the Freshers' Fair.

***

Rhys was bored. She wished they could lure unsuspecting Freshers to join the societies without the draw of sweets, fridge magnets, and pens. One of the Old Boys' Clubs was even running a prize draw for an iPad Pro in exchange for data-harvesting the names and contact details of these unsuspecting kids. *It shouldn't be allowed.*

She leaned back in her chair, arms crossed over her chest, and raised her eyebrow at the student who had just done a third pass of the table to pick up another free pencil. *What's he even going to do with them all?* Rhys thought back to five years ago when she'd moved house and threw away the ten-year-old pens with the faded logo of her undergrad university on them. *I hope you carry those pencils round to every house you ever live in, mate.* She sent the silent curse out into the universe, picturing how many times these logoed pencils would see the inside of moving boxes in their lifetime.

She snapped her attention back to a student at the table who actually stopped to ask an intelligent question about the sign language club.

Scarlet couldn't believe her luck. Dr Gorgeous was sitting at the sign language table. Enrolling in that club was the main reason she wanted to come to the Fair, and now she had the added bonus of seeing Rhys. *Two birds, one stone.* Unlike Jessica, she wasn't all that interested in the pens and pencils the different clubs and societies were giving out. She wanted to join some clubs to meet new people.

She loitered at the opposite stall. *First-Aid — very useful*, until the students around the sign language table moved on.

"Um. Hi, Dr Hunter." Scarlet took her chance and swooped in before the space in front of the stall filled again.

"Coffee Girl. Hello again." Rhys made her hand into a C shape and mimed tipping a cup to her mouth before swiping her forefinger along her cheek. At Scarlet's bemused expression she explained the sign for "coffee" and then the sign for "girl."

"Some people use a sign that represents them, or just their initial, instead of fingerspelling their name."

That made sense. Amy used the pinkie promise sign for her name. It was the sign for S. Scarlet had watched a YouTube video about fingerspelling. It was a special feeling having her own sign. She smiled and her cheeks turned an embarrassing shade of pink. *Dr Gorgeous not only remembered me, but she gave me a nickname.* Scarlet's heart beat hard inside her chest.

"So Coffee Girl, do you want to join us to learn some sign language?"

"I do, and my name is Scarlet." Scarlet said, making the sign for S.

"I think I like 'Coffee Girl' better," Rhys said with a grin.

———

Two hours later, the girls sat under a tree at the edge of the green. They were eating cupcakes with the university logo on top, printed on sugar paper.

"I don't think it should be called the Freshers' Fair," Jessica said, folding her paper case into a small triangle. "They should just call it 'Cakes and Condoms'!"

"Absolutely." Kemi agreed, her mouth still full of cake.

"That sounds like a 1950s motherhood class from *Call the Midwife.*" Lily chuckled. Scarlet picked at the icing on top of her cake. She laughed along with her friends, but her mind was on seeing Rhys again. She felt like they had a connection. Rhys hadn't treated her like a child. She was pretty sure the older woman had been flirting with her.

Chapter Nine

Soft music played through the restaurant at a tasteful volume, relaxing the diners and blending pleasingly with the low chatter of voices. It wasn't crowded, and the waiters moved easily between the tables, bringing food and drink out at a quick pace.

Marie fluttered her eyelashes across the table at Greg The Dentist. Things with him were going better than she had planned. If she had her way, she would get a proposal from him by Christmas. It couldn't come soon enough. The bank declined her last credit card application and the electricity payment bounced, again. *Perhaps Scarlet will lend me some money from her student loan?* She discreetly tapped her phone to life next to her place setting, still smiling over at Greg while she messaged Scarlet to see if her loan money had arrived.

Scarlet's reply came before the waiter served their next course.

Yes, money went into my account on the first day of term xx

Marie smiled and quickly texted back.

thts great d'ling. cud you log on2 online banking 2pay elec bill?

Mum I need that money to pay my rent.

And you don't need to type in text speak, texts aren't limited to a certain number of characters anymore x

I'll call you tomorrow mum xx

Just this once d'ling? xoxo

Marie laughed along with what Greg was saying and eyed the nearly empty bottle of wine. Greg saw her looking around for their waiter. "Do you want another wine, sweetheart?"

"Actually, darling, I think a nice glass of Cognac would go down superbly with dessert."

"Of course, of course." Greg caught the waiter's eye

and ordered their drinks. He wanted to make Marie happy. She was so different from his ex-wife. She was fun-loving and liked to indulge in good food and drink. Paula, his ex, always watched what he spent, and insisted on putting a large chunk of his wages into a private pension scheme instead of enjoying it now. She claimed it was vital to save for retirement. He thought she was paranoid.

Marie looked longingly at the cards in his wallet when he pulled it out to pay for dinner. "Greg, darling, what do you say to a nice little city break? We could do a long weekend somewhere in Europe? I'll have a look, shall I, and book something for us? You can transfer me the money and your passport number, and I'll sort it all out."

Greg grinned adoringly at the charming woman as she toyed with the long necklace that dipped into her cleavage. She smiled back. She would tell him the holiday cost more than it really did and use the extra to pay some of her bills.

***

Music pumped from the wifi speaker in Scarlet's bedroom. Each of the girls had one of the small devices. Jessica had logged into her music streaming account on the smart TV in the lounge so they could all listen anywhere in the house. Scarlet didn't recognise the song; it was something one of her housemates must've added to the *Girls Night Out* playlist.

She was getting ready for the legendary Freshers' Week pub crawl, dancing in front of the wardrobe in just her underwear.

When her phone vibrated on the desk, alerting her to a text, she looked at her phone in disgust. *I've only been gone two weeks and already mum is in some kind of trouble.* She thought about turning on her iPad and logging into her mum's online banking account, but she took a deep breath instead and put the phone back down, returning to her open wardrobe and surveying her outfit options.

Jessica insisted the pub crawl was not to be missed. They would meet at the designated starting point and make their way round the pubs and bars offering the best student deals. The goal was obviously to get as drunk as possible and then spend the weekend recovering.

Scarlet wasn't really into getting drunk. Watching her mum's relationship with alcohol gave her a healthy respect for it. The pub crawl held other attractions for her: socialising with her friends, meeting new people, and learning her way around town. They would also find out which pubs served food, which nights had bands playing live music, and which clubs had upcoming theme nights. *Sussing out where the gay venues were wouldn't hurt either.* She wasn't into "The

Scene" but it was nice to know where she could find other queer people. *I know I don't need to get drunk to have a good time tonight.*

She pulled out several tops that would go well with her favourite pair of tight black jeans. Holding them up in turn, she tried to decide which to wear.

She wondered whether she would see Dr Gorgeous while she was out. Rhys seemed like the sort of fun person who would go out on a Friday night, not sit at home writing lesson plans.

Would she like me better in the figure-hugging red top that covers more skin or the low-cut silver one? Hmm. Which one? Mum would vote for the low-cut one, always erring on the side of cleavage. But I know I look hot in the red one, and Rhys strikes me as preferring a more classy look.

The silver top was returned to the wardrobe.

She laid the red top out on the bed and shimmied into her jeans. Smoothing her hands down her thighs, she admired herself in the mirror. The black material was like a second skin, and when she pulled the top over her head it clung to her curves.

Now all she needed was for Lily to finish in the bathroom so she could clean her teeth. *Just in case there's a chance of any kissing happening tonight.*

Once her breath was fresh and her lipgloss reapplied, Scarlet made her way downstairs to join the others. She would deal with whatever was going on with her mother tomorrow.

———

Throughout the evening Scarlet kept an eye out for Rhys. A couple of times her heartbeat picked up when she thought she'd spotted her in the crowd of pulsing bodies. Each time she danced closer, and each time she was disappointed to discover it wasn't the gorgeous Dr Hunter. *I'm not drunk, my eyes are playing tricks on me because I want to see her. It's just wishful thinking.*

She laughed with her friends, and she danced. In some of the bars the music pounded, in others they were able to chat. Kemi didn't drink, so she was voted their responsible adult. Jessica and Lily took the opportunity to let loose, trusting their friend to keep them safe.

Scarlet had a pleasant buzz going by the time they reached the third pub. She was talking to Kemi next to the bar, when Lily pulled a girl over to their group.

"Scarlet!" Lily shouted over the music, "This is, um—"

"Carla," the other girl supplied.

"Yeah, Carla," Lily slurred slightly. "So, you and, um, Carla. You and Carla. You have something in common."

"Oh?" Scarlet asked.

"Yep," Lily nodded gleefully. "You both like to shag

chicks! So, y'know," She gestured between them and wiggled her eyebrows.

"Okay, Lil, time to drink some water." Scarlet handed her off to Kemi and turned to Carla. "I'm really sorry about her."

"S'okay," Carla drawled, not quite as drunk as Lily, "So, Scarlet-who-likes-to-shag-chicks, wanna dance?"

For the next couple of songs they moved together on the dancefloor. She even gave Carla a cheeky kiss on the lips when she went back to her friends, but subconsciously Scarlet was always on the lookout for Rhys.

———

Meanwhile, Rhys sat at home writing a new lesson plan. Her stomach rumbled, and she unplugged her laptop, carrying it from her office to the living room. She left it on the coffee table while she grabbed a banana from the fruit bowl. Then she plopped down on the sofa and started typing again. A small wiry head snuffled out of the blanket in the middle of the sofa and rested on the keyboard. "You want to help do you, madame? Ok, have at it."

She ruffled the dog's head affectionately, then had to hit the "undo" button to get rid of the extra characters the dog's nose had pressed.

Chapter Ten

The next morning was bright and sunny, as if September suddenly remembered it was indeed closer to summer than winter. The sunlight streamed in through the curtains Scarlet forgot to close the night before, waking her up far earlier than she really wanted considering how late she got in. She had consumed a modest amount of alcohol but she hadn't fallen prey to the £1 shots being thrown at the Freshers as they drank their way through the classic rite of passage.

A large glass of water sat on her bedside table, and she reached out to drink it all before collapsing back onto her bed. She stared up at the ceiling and fiddled with the papery neon wristband that had granted her access to the various places on the pub crawl route. She pulled on the band, and it cut into the skin of her wrist.

She gave up, deciding scissors would be required to remove it.

Not seeing Rhys last night disappointed Scarlet. Of course, she had no real reason to expect her to be there. A few tutors and third-year students chaperoned the pub crawl, wearing their purple neon vests with the university logo on the back. *I just wish Dr Gorgeous had been one of them.*

Scarlet felt a magnetic pull whenever she was near Rhys. *She's confident in her own skin and so very charming. Totally my type.*

Scarlet definitely had a type. Her last girlfriend had been cute in a soft butch sort of way that made Scarlet's heart race. She had been on the ladies' rugby team, and Scarlet spent far too many cold wet Sundays watching from the sidelines. *If that's not commitment then I don't know what is.* Unfortunately, that level of commitment didn't go both ways. They broke up during the summer when Megan announced she was deferring her university place and taking a gap year to travel around America. Scarlet felt a twinge of regret that she wasn't taking a gap year to travel the world. Megan suggested Scarlet could join her, but there was no way she could afford to go. Plus, she knew her mother would never have been able to cope with her daughter in a different country.

Scarlet knew Megan hadn't been *the one* for her, but it still hurt to think she'd been left behind so easily. That was how her relationships panned out — Scarlet putting in the majority of the effort.

Marie made an unsuccessful attempt to disguise her glee at the breakup. She tried to coach her daughter from a young age to "marry up," being of the belief that she—and by association, her daughter—deserved to be treated to the best things in life. Marie didn't care much about how they came by those things. She moulded herself into the perfect second wife, moving from husband to husband, an expert in convincing the men they had been stifled by their first wives. Then she would tag along on their coattails while she manipulated them into a spending spree. When they tired of her, or when the money ran out, she simply moved on to the next one.

One of Scarlet's earliest memories was her mother telling her to find a good husband. And by "good," of course, she meant rich. By the time Scarlet was fifteen and bringing girlfriends home from school, Marie changed the advice to where her daughter might meet a rich woman — the squash club rather than the golf club — apparently rich lesbians didn't play golf, according to Marie.

As it was Saturday Scarlet hoped for a nice lie-in before spending the weekend with her new friends. There was a quiz night at the Students' Union at six o'clock they planned to go to. That gave them plenty of time to recover from the pub crawl the night before.

Scarlet trudged over to the window and yanked the curtains shut. She contemplated going down to the kitchen to make coffee but decided her bed was a better prospect. Back under the covers, she reached for her phone, fully intending to scroll through eBay for a secondhand coffee pod machine for her bedroom.

When she unlocked her phone it opened up the text conversation with her mum from the previous night. *Argh.*

An hour later, Scarlet sat cross-legged on her bed with her phone and iPad open in front of her. She went back and forth between the screens: her mother's online banking and several utility bill company websites. Payments were going out to credit agencies, but she didn't have the login details to access those accounts. *Shit. What has mum been doing? Probably paying the minimum amount off her credit cards so they don't cut her off while letting the utility bills bounce.*

So much for her nice relaxing weekend. She picked up her phone and called her mum.

Marie's modus operandi was simple: buy things on credit to put across a certain lifestyle to the man she was after. It was important to cultivate the relationship first so she could then use his money to pay off the debts. It was a fine balance, but she usually got the timing just right. Thank goodness Marie inherited the family home from her mother. At least there was no mortgage to worry about.

She sat on the sofa with Suzanne, who was showing her photos of her latest holiday. She looked at the picture of Suzanne and her new husband, dressed up to go to dinner on the cruise ship, with envy. "That dress is simply stunning, darling. Wherever did you get it?"

"Oh, that? I think it's a John Roche. I can have a look at the label when I get home."

Marie's phone buzzed. She glanced at the screen and saw it was Scarlet calling her. She rolled her eyes and rejected the call, putting the phone in her pocket.

"More coffee, Suze?" Marie headed to the kitchen where she could add a bit of something extra to her cup.

Scarlet tried unsuccessfully to get in touch with her mother all weekend. She called and sent texts asking her mum to call her back. On Sunday she even phoned her mother's elderly neighbour Mrs Kent, but the kindly pensioner told her that her hip was acting up so she hadn't ventured outside her house for a few days. The hedge between their houses meant that she couldn't see whether Marie's car was on the driveway from her window.

By the time Monday rolled around, Scarlet was worried.

She had a seminar to attend in the early afternoon, but once that finished she was sure she was going to have to bite the bullet and drive home to check on Marie. Going home offered the advantage of also being able to check on Mrs Kent while she was at it. *Maybe I'll take her round some shopping.*

It was five o'clock by the time Scarlet got to her mum's house. She pulled into the driveway of the three storey Victorian. In her usual parking spot sat a shiny black Mercedes she didn't recognise.

She rolled her eyes. *I guess we all have our own unique type. At least we can rely on the consistency of the men mum chooses.*

She considered reversing off the driveway and going to get Mrs Kent that shopping, but, as she thought about leaving, she saw the net curtain twitch in the bay window. Her mother knew she was here.

Screwing her face up, a headache already forming, she parked behind her mother's Audi. She wanted him to be able to leave easily if he wanted to, so she was careful not to block in his car.

She opened the driver's door and put on the most genuine smile she could muster. One thing was clear, she wouldn't be able to confront her mum about her finances while her new man in the house.

Chapter Eleven

University life was getting into full swing as the first few weeks passed. Scarlet and her friends settled into the routines and trials of living together, and they'd only run out of toilet paper once! Lectures were interesting, and the workshops were fun. As Rhys predicted, Scarlet's tutor sessions with Dr Baker were as dull as dishwater. More than once Scarlet found her mind wandering during his seminars. Her mother was often the focus of her preoccupation, taking up far more head space than she should, and things between them were still stilted.

At least Greg The Dentist is keeping mum busy so I get a break from her. He seems like a nice enough chap. Completely typical of the men mum goes after: not long divorced, and now he isn't tied down to his wife and kids, mum's busy showing him the lifestyle he can have.The whole situation makes me feel sick. She's my mum, I can't call her a con-artist; but she's not a truly loving girl-friend either. I'd feel sorry for these men, but surely they can't be stupid enough to think she loves them?

Attending the lectures given by Rhys had been the only time she got a break from all the Marie thoughts swirling around her brain. *Dr Gorgeous is the only thing that can get mum out of my head. Rhys. I need to call her by her name. The first sign language class is due to start at the end of October, and I can't accidentally blurt out that nickname in front of her.*

For now, she would lust after her from afar, but the sign language class would give her a chance to interact with Dr Rhys Hunter in person.

The leaflets she picked up from Rhys at the Fresh-ers' Fair explained that the town of Dalesbury had a well-established Deaf community. One hundred and fifty years ago a school for the Deaf was founded on the site where the university now stood. The original Victo-rian building, Creasy Hall, had been absorbed into the university campus.

I wondered whether Amy's involved in the local Deaf community? Perhaps helps out with the sign language class? Is it presumptive to assume that, just because she's deaf? I guess it's a bit like asking someone who lives in London if they know the queen. It would be rude to ask her.

. . .

Standing at the podium, Rhys looked out into the sea of First-Year faces. Her lecture just finished, and she asked if they had any questions. She knew the sheer volume of students could be intimidating to some; usually the same few spoke up in the lecture theatre. Most were happy to leave it to their fellow students, preferring to ask their questions one-to-one while everyone else was filing out or waiting to discuss the lecture in the seminar the following day.

Rhys finished answering the questions from the predictable few students who had the confidence to speak in front of their peers. She dismissed the lecture and slowly began disconnecting her laptop from the cables on the podium. She generally found taking her time before leaving the theatre made her accessible to the more shy students.

She rolled up her charger cable and stuffed it into the pocket of her bag. Coffee Girl was sitting in the third row, and she made no move to leave her seat. Rhys glanced at her before making eye contact with the sandy-haired boy walking towards her.

"Dr Hunter, do you have a minute?"

"Sure mate, and it's Rhys alright? Now, how can I help?"

Several times now she had felt like Scarlet was hanging around at the end of her lectures, perhaps trying to get up the courage to ask her a question. She hadn't seemed overly shy when they had spoken at the Freshers' Fair, but perhaps she wasn't confident in her academic voice. Rhys was just the person to help with that.

Scarlet suddenly snapped out of her daydream. *Had Dr Gorgeous finished speaking? Rhys... her name is Rhys.* She couldn't help being lulled into some decidedly naughty thoughts about *tall, dark and- Rhys, her name is Rhys.* Scarlet's thoughts really weren't on her coursework right now. She swung back and forth between concern over what her mother was up to and warm, squishy thoughts about her lecturer.

It was definitely more pleasant to be thinking of Rhys than Marie.

Rhys handing over a coffee cup with a wink. Rhys smiling and signing her special nickname. Rhys' hand cupping her face, her fingers sliding back into her hair, bringing their lips together-

Oh, shit.

Scarlet jolted herself out of her thoughts. Quickly gathering up her iPad, she scooted to the end of the row of seats, escaping from the lecture theatre while Rhys was busy with the student who was animatedly talking to her.

Outside the double doors, Scarlet stopped and pressed her hands to her face. Her cheeks were burning. She hoped no one she knew walked past. More than anything, she hoped Rhys didn't walk through those doors right then. But this was Scarlet's life, so of course the doors swung open and Rhys pulled up short just before walking into her back.

"Coffee Girl, hey! Were you waiting for me?"

It feels like I've been waiting for you my whole life.

Scarlet was relieved she managed to find the self control from somewhere not to voice her thoughts out loud. "I, um—"

"It seemed like you wanted to ask me a question back there?"

Yes — will you take me out for coffee, or dinner, or home to meet your parents?! Shut up, shut up.

"Yes. No. I mean, not really. I just wondered—" Scarlet pressed her fingers to the bridge of her nose and turned her head away.

"Do you want to grab a coffee, Coffee Girl?"

Swoon. It's like she can read my mind. I hope she can't. How embarrassing would it be if she could just look at me and know what I had been thinking about her earlier?

Chapter Twelve

S carlet gazed across the table at Rhys, trying to make it seem like she wasn't staring at the most stunning woman she'd ever had coffee with.

She didn't want this to be Rhys' first proper impression of her. A starry-eyed First-Year, her lips slightly parted and her pupils dilated. If you opened a human biology textbook to the page about the physiological signs of arousal, there would be a tiny picture of Scarlet's face as it was right at that moment.

They went to the café next to the admin building. It was smaller than the Student Union and quieter, much better for talking across the table. Scarlet ordered her usual large mocha and started dumping several sachets of sugar into her cup as soon as she sat down. Rhys ordered a black Americano and only put in one sugar. "Woah, Coffee Girl, it's a miracle you could drink that coffee I gave you a couple of weeks ago."

"It had caffeine, that's all I needed." Scarlet distractedly reached for her last sugar sachet and tore it open while smiling at Rhys. Before she knew what happened the sugar granules were all over the table. *Oh, God.*

"You seem very nervous, are you worried about something?"

"No, not nervous. I'm just a bit jittery—probably too much caffeine."

"Well, you haven't actually had any of your coffee yet. So I'm wondering... Do I make you nervous, Scarlet?"

"What? No! You're—" *Perfect. Amazing. Sexy as hell.* "You seem really easy to talk to Dr Hunter."

"Call me 'Rhys,' remember? Dr Hunter is my grandfather."

"Oh? What's he a doctor of?"

"He's a medical doctor. He's retired now. He and my Gran moved to a tiny village in Cornwall a few years ago. It's a much nicer pace of life for them."

"Do you get to see them often?"

"Not as much as I'd like, but, yes. Their new house came with a little holiday cottage they rent out; Gran loves to dote on their guests. She makes homemade scones and cakes. I go and stay when I can."

"It sounds lovely. Can you smuggle me there in your suitcase next time?" They both laughed, and Scarlet tucked the image of going to an idyllic little getaway with Rhys away in her mind to fantasize about later.

The ice broken, Scarlet relaxed into the conversation while they drank their coffee. It was nice to sit like this and pretend Rhys wasn't her teacher. But instead, someone she could have a proper mature conversation with, someone who treated her like an equal rather than a child.

Scarlet puzzled Rhys. *It's like she's putting on an act when underneath she's self-conscious and unsure of herself. I hope I can help bring her out of her shell a bit more.*

Rhys could tell Scarlet lacked confidence in herself, which was not unusual for a teenager just becoming an adult. With Scarlet, though, it seemed to run deeper than the usual ungainliness of young adults and more an undercurrent of self-doubt. Rhys wondered what, or who, could have caused Scarlet's confidence to be so low. Students usually fell into two categories: young adults who still felt like children, searching to find their place in the word; or those with an overconfident "nothing can hurt me" attitude. *Scarlet definitely falls into the first group.*

"So, how have you been finding your workload?"

Rhys decided that was the safest line of questioning to begin trying to work out what was bothering Scarlet.

"To be honest with you, it's not as straightforward as I expected." She fiddled with the empty sugar packets, idly shredding them into a pile of confetti. "I was really good at school. I got good grades and I didn't need to do much revision. I didn't realise it would be so different here."

Rhys nodded in understanding, "Has Dr Baker given you some suggestions? There are lots of resources that might help you. There's a quiz you can do to workout what style of learner you are."

"He has tried, but I had the same problem reading through the study guides as I have with the actual coursework." She looked up, and Rhys saw a flash of sadness cross her face before she smiled. "I have been enjoying it though, especially your lectures. They're so interesting, which makes it much easier to take in the information."

"You're right, Scarlet. In my experience, students do find the work easier when they're enjoying it.

"Well, I know my opinion doesn't count for much in the grand scheme of things, but I think you're doing a great job, Rhys."

"Of course your opinion counts, don't ever let anyone tell you it doesn't. And thank you." *Who's made you think so poorly of yourself, Scarlet? Perhaps this isn't just a case of not understanding the work, is something else going on for you?*

Rhys could tell Scarlet was still putting on a front, trying to sweep the real issue under the rug. But she didn't want to push her too hard and cause her to shy away before getting any help.

I already knew Dr Baker's engagement needs some work. But I'll have to arrange a meeting to talk through ways he could help Scarlet engage with her work. It would be easy to let him fly under the radar for the next few years until he decides to retire. But that's not the way I want to manage my department.

Chapter Thirteen

Walking home from campus, Scarlet couldn't believe she had actually been out for a drink with Rhys Hunter. Granted, it was just coffee, but still. She would indulge in her fantasy for a little while longer, imagining the setting was more romantic, their conversation had lasted longer, that they had been on a date. *I hope Rhys didn't realise anything was wrong apart from my issues with the coursework. I can't let her realise there's anything more to it than that. What if she realises that I'm not good enough for her?*

She pulled out her phone and typed a quick text to her mother, telling her she had been out for coffee with the charming lecturer. She tucked the phone back into her pocket before Marie could reply; she didn't want to stand on the pavement jabbing at her phone screen when she could snuggle up on the sofa with a cup of tea and the chatter of her housemates around her.

If Marie decided to grace her daughter with her attention then Scarlet would reply in her own time. Well, probably, she could keep telling herself that it was now her choice to engage with her mother on her own terms, but the truth of the matter was the chime of her phone was like her mother snapping her fingers, and Scarlet always had a Pavlovian response. Scarlet would have to respond; she would be responding before she even realised the phone was in her hand. Why couldn't she get some nice, healthy distance from her mother? She was still working on that. She would have to work harder.

Marie smiled smugly down at her phone. *That little madam thought she was so high and mighty, saying she didn't want to reel in a rich girlfriend. Well, perhaps things looked different now she was out on her own, without the security of living in the family home.*

Marie considered typing a reply but decided to let Scarlet stew without mummy's advice for a bit. Besides, Suzanne was coming over to help her choose her outfit for the charity board's afternoon tea next week. As the charity's chairwoman, she would make sure she put across the very best impression. The people she would meet, friends and relatives of the other board members, really were important connections to make. She might even meet a man in an even better financial position than Greg The Dentist.

Being on the charity board was a great little hobby for Marie. Not only did it allow her to meet and mix with the class of people she aspired to be, but it also allowed her the guise of having a job. She couldn't allow Scarlet to find out where her money really came from. It was true that she received a monthly deposit into her account that looked for all intents and purposes like a wage. It didn't come from her work on the charity board. The source of her monthly income was much less legitimate. *Legitimacy, that was the operative word, wasn't it?*

Marie had received a monthly allowance since before Scarlet was born. It wasn't a child maintenance payment; it was more like hush money. Scarlet didn't know who her father was, and her mother wanted to keep it that way. The money bought her silence.

Marie went to work as a personal assistant in The City when she was twenty-five. She was PA to the CEO's son in a large banking firm. He was ten years her senior, and he and his wife had small children. Marie soon had him taking her out to fancy lunches, bestowing him with the undivided attention that his wife was too busy to give him. Their affair lasted for a couple of years and ended when Marie told him she was pregnant. His father, the CEO, was a devoted family man who would not have tolerated his son's infidelity. Fearing he would be removed from his father's company, he forced Marie to resign. She left with a monthly allowance and the threat of being cut off if she divulged the affair and the baby to anyone.

It had been easy enough to tell Scarlet her arsehole father walked out on them when she was a baby. Marie always refused to talk about him.

Marie pulled several outfits out of the large wardrobe and laid them across the bed. She retrieved her phone, thought about replying to her daughter, but opened Google instead.

University Lecturer Salary

She was soon scanning down the results, shaking her head and tutting. *Didn't Scarlet say that this woman was the head of her course? That would be a slight improvement. She must be much older than her daughter.*

Marie cleared the search and started again.

University Department Head Salary

She cringed. Not much better than the previous results. Scarlet would have them be destitute rather than buck her ideas up and follow her mother's advice. Perhaps this woman could be coached into loftier career aspirations, and perhaps a pretty young lady like her daughter could be just the incentive needed. A little bit of ego stroking and a few well-placed whispers in someone's ear could do wonders for a person's prospects. In Marie's experience, it was easy to manipulate lovers into going for a promotion to impress her. Why shouldn't that work for her daughter too?

With a smirk, Marie typed again.

University Dean Salary

Of course, it was far easier and quicker to find a target who was already loaded. Scarlet could work her way up to that, though. Marie wasn't completely heartless. Her daughter could have it so much worse; at least her mother wasn't insisting that she pursue a man.

Marie nodded to herself, happy in the knowledge she was a modern woman and a good mother. She poured herself a drink from the decanter in her bedroom and settled on the window seat to wait for Suzanne.

Chapter Fourteen

Reading week came and went, and the second half of the term ushered in proper Autumn weather. Scarlet trudged home after a full day of lectures and seminars. It was getting colder, and she pulled her coat tightly around herself to keep out the worst of the chill. She had her first BSL class tonight, so she was planning to nip home for a warm bowl of soup and a crusty roll for dinner before she headed out again. For the last few weeks she had been practising her sign alphabet, fingerspelling names of places and people.

She was excited about the class, more excited than she'd been for a few weeks.

She went back home during reading week and things with her mother were tense. Several times she tried to speak with her about her finances, but Marie was a master of turning the conversation around in her favour. Nothing was wrong. She was in love with her new man and only wanted to talk about happy things. Why was Scarlet trying to bring the mood down in the house?

Scarlet returned to uni in a bad mood. She was concerned, but she worried if she pushed her mother too far, she might change the passwords to her online banking and then Scarlet would be completely in the dark as to what her mother was doing.

After she ate her soup, Scarlet thought about trying to call her mum to talk about what happened last week. She picked her phone up and scrolled to Marie's number. Then she thought better of it and took a bit of extra time getting ready for the class. Rhys was going to be there after all. It was a good use of her time to make herself look nice. She wondered what sort of look Rhys found appealing as she made her way up to her bedroom. Personally, she wasn't a fan of wearing heavy makeup herself, but Marie ensured she knew how to put on a classy face of products for the right occasion. This evening she opted for an understated look. She wanted to look nice, without it seeming like she was trying too hard.

Jessica offered to come with Scarlet to the first class, but Scarlet said she would be fine. In truth, she worried she would become a bumbling mess in front of Rhys. Jessica would take one look at her and realise she was catching feels for her lecturer. It was better to keep her feelings hidden. They felt warm and precious, a small ball in her chest that flared to life every time she saw Rhys. She didn't think Jessica would make fun of her, but she didn't want to be told how much of a bad idea it was to be hopelessly lusting after the older woman.

Creasy Hall had old casement windows which didn't keep out the cold like double glazing would have. The other students kept their coats on, waiting for the room to warm up. Scarlet was hot; she discarded her coat as soon as she arrived. In the back of her mind, she knew this was her body's reaction to thinking about being in a room with Rhys. Then she was thinking about being in a different sort of room with Rhys. A smaller room with fewer people and a bed in it. Her cheeks burned.

She pressed her hands to her face, hoping that no one would notice how red she was sure she'd become.

Scarlet's phone buzzed in her pocket, and she groaned. *Mum would choose now to re-establish contact, with only a few minutes before class is due to start.* She pulled out her phone, only to be pleasantly surprised to see Jessica's name on the screen, *Good luck hun! We all hope you have a good time.* It made a change to receive a nice message and not a demand of some kind from her mother.

The first thing Rhys did when she arrived was to make introductions. She had two older students with her, and she explained they were part of the university's

Deaf community and would assist with the class. All the while she spoke she also signed. It looked so fluid and beautiful, and Scarlet couldn't take her eyes off of her.

Rhys instructed them to push the tables back and move their chairs into a circle, explaining that doing so would make it easier to see everyone else's hands and expressions. It fascinated Scarlet to learn how much body language and facial expressions went into sign language. As it was the first session, Rhys explained the things they would do in the class. "As we progress, you'll get to choose which signs we'll cover. We can do all sorts of topics, so it's best to do the ones that interest you most. I'm going to hand round a pad of paper each week and if there's a situation or topic that you'd like to cover, then write it down. During the course of your everyday activities, I bet you'll come across things you'll think would be handy to know."

They each took a photocopied sheet with the finger-spelling alphabet on it, and together they went through each letter. Scarlet had been practising these already, and she relaxed into the class. One of the older students, Kai, showed them how to sign the question "What is your name?"

They practised asking the person next to them their name and replying. Then Rhys passed around some flashcards with famous names on them, and they practised trying to guess what was on the other person's card. Scarlet managed to guess her partner's new name was

Mary Shelley, and it took slightly longer for them to guess she was Neil Armstrong. It was fun, and everyone was laughing by the end.

Before it was time to leave, Rhys gave them each a sheet of paper with some question words and key signs on it. She ran through them, then asked the group to practise signing them before the next class. "Next week we'll look at how to sign a question and we'll do some more fingerspelling. Some words have to be finger-spelled because they don't have their own sign, so we can practise more next time with place names."

Everyone filed out of the room, but Scarlet took her time gathering her things together. She looked around and saw her chance to linger just a bit longer and poten-tially get a chance to talk to Rhys. She picked up her chair and started putting the classroom furniture back to normal.

Rhys finished organising the spare handouts back into their plastic wallets and slipped them into her bag. She smiled over at Scarlet and came over to help lift a table back into the middle of the room. "Thank you, Scarlet. You didn't have to do this. I'm sure you'd prefer to be getting back home and out of this cold, dark weather as soon as possible."

"I figured if I helped it would get both of us home quicker. I mean, I'm assuming you need to get home? I'm not in any rush, I—"

"Scarlet, I'd love to sit down and have a catch up

with you, but it is getting late tonight. Why don't we meet up for a coffee after my lecture on Thursday morning?"

"That sounds great." Scarlet tried not to let the disappointment leak through into her voice. Coffee in the middle of the day didn't have the same intimate feel as going out for a drink in the evening, but she was happy Rhys wanted to spend time with her.

Rhys gave her a warm smile as she held open the door for them both to leave the classroom, flicking the light off before letting the heavy door swing shut.

Scarlet felt positive as she walked back home. *It might be cold, wet and windy, but I feel better than I have all week. I really enjoyed the class, and it was so nice to spend time with Rhys.* She considered pulling out her phone to check for messages from her mother, but she pushed the urge back down. For a little while, she would hold on to this happy feeling before she let the worries of the last few weeks roll back in again.

Perhaps she could find something here at uni that would sustain her emotionally and let her feel able to take a step further away from Marie's orbit.

Marie stood in the bay window looking out at the rainy driveway. There was a dry patch of gravel where Greg's car had been parked. He had taken a call from his ex-wife to say their son had been tackled hard at football and might have a broken bone. He'd flung on his coat and raced out of there to meet them at A and E.

Marie clutched the glass in her hand and tried not to scream in frustration. They had been getting on really well, and she knew his lease was nearly up on the flat he had been renting. She had been planning to ply him with good food and drink tonight and then suggest he not renew his lease and move in with her instead. That would at least give her the security of being able to get him to pay the utility bills.

She realised her glass was empty and staggered back over to the coffee table to retrieve the bottle. As she plopped back down on the sofa, she felt something hard poking into her hip. She twisted to look and smiled. Greg's wallet must have fallen out of his trouser pocket.

She flipped it open and traced her finger lovingly over the cards. She had become a master of the small unnoticeable purchases, ones that the card's owner wouldn't notice as additions to their monthly statement. She pulled out the first card and opened up her laptop.

He owed her something for his abrupt departure this evening. He didn't know it yet but he was about to buy Marie a present to cheer her up.

Chapter Fifteen

"Mum? Are you listening to me?"

Marie rolled her eyes, glad her daughter couldn't see her over the phone. Sometimes it was just best to let Scarlet prattle on about all the boring things she wanted to talk about and then pretend the phone signal dipped.

"Yes, darling, of course I am." *White wine, Brie, Stilton, chutney, red wine, crackers, coffee.* Marie mentally went through her shopping list.

"So then she asked me out for coffee!"

"Really, darling? That's nice." Marie tried not to sound sarcastic. "Do you know how much she earns? What sort of car does she drive? Does she rent or does she own her house? Big mortgage?"

"Mum!" Scarlet seemed shocked at her mother's sudden swing from indifference to interrogation. Marie shrugged. *I don't care what she thinks, I need to know what sort of prospects this teacher has. I'm not allowing her to cultivate another dead-end relationship like she did with that Megan girl.*

"These are important questions you need to get out of the way right at the beginning of a relationship, Scarlet. Not soppy things like 'are you a dog or cat person?' You need to get to the heart of the matter. Where does she see her career in five years? Does she pay into a private pension? That's money she could be spending on you now."

"Mum, stop it."

"No, you listen to me young lady. If this woman isn't up to our standards, the lifestyle we deserve, then just shag her, get her out of your system and move on."

"Mother! I'm not listening to this!"

"You *will* listen. I've taken care of you for your entire life. I've fed you and clothed you. I've worked hard for us to survive, to keep our house, to keep us comfortable and happy. Now I need you to show me you've learnt something—anything—from me. You wouldn't want me to have to sell our house, would you?"

"Mum, has something happened? Have you taken out a loan against the house? Do you need me to come home?"

"No, darling, you stay there and go on your date with your teacher."

Marie hung up, not hearing Scarlet's exclamation

she was an adult, and that Rhys was more than her teacher.

Scarlet wanted to throw something. Her phone case creaked in her hand as she gripped it a bit too tightly. She really mustn't throw the phone across the room. *Do other people's mums speak to them like this?*

They must do, right?

Mum just wants what's best for me.

Of course mum loves me. Doesn't she?

Scarlet pulled herself back from allowing her thoughts to drift into the realms of her mother not loving her. *That's just not possible is it? All parents love their children; they just have different ways of showing it. I do so much for mum. How could she not love me?*

The little voice in the back of her mind, which sounded a bit like Amy, whispered, *She loves what you do for her. Please see that.*

She allowed herself to escape into a fantasy of her and Rhys, full after eating one too many homemade scones, walking along an empty beach in Cornwall. Only the salty air stopped their breath from coming out in clouds. They would be wearing big coats, Rhys would try to wrap her arms around her but the thick layers would make it impossible. They would laugh and the sound would echo across the sea. Then Rhys would kiss her.

The email alert sounded on her phone. She looked down at the screen and cursed. This time, she did throw the phone. Luckily, it hit a pile of laundry on her chair.

The automatic email reminded her to upload the electronic copy of her coursework to the university's website by 10pm tomorrow, where it would be run against their plagiarism software. The assignment was a 3,000 word essay. She wrote about 700 words during Reading Week and then promptly forgot about it with the stress of trying to talk to Marie about their family finances.

Wouldn't that just be the icing on the cake? Failing my course and having to slink off home to mum with my tail between my legs. She'd love that wouldn't she? Having me back to do her bidding. She'd find a woman for me; one she's vetted and approves of her bank balance and investment portfolio. Someone with a high flying career who wouldn't have time for me.

Scarlet slid down to the floor, her head buried in her hands. She felt sick.

Chapter Sixteen

Scarlet holed up in the computer suite in the library basement the next day, skipping the arranged study group session to cram 3,000 words out of her head and onto the bright, white screen. Her eyes were sore and her mouth was dry; she long since finished the water she had brought with her. At 8pm, with 500 words to go and two hours until the submission deadline, Scarlet decided to take a quick break to grab a bottle of Coke from the vending machine in the lobby. She could get her caffeine fix and pop to the loo at the same time.

As she climbed the stairs, she heard a dog snuffling. It confused her for a minute until she remembered Peggy. It was just after the closing time of the library, only the computer suites in the basement were accessible after 8pm. Amy must have been closing up the library and was about to head home. Scarlet hurried up the stairs, hoping to say goodnight.

As her head got level with the top of the stairs she froze. Peggy had given an excited yip, and Amy gave the hand signal that released her companion. Peggy bounded across the lobby to the figure who had just walked through the entrance.

The terrier waited for Rhys to make a fuss of her then danced in a circle before prancing back over to Amy. The two women signed to each other as Rhys closed the distance between them completely, taking Amy in her arms. Scarlet couldn't look away as the woman she wanted bent her head slightly and gave Amy a soft hello kiss. Their eyes briefly closed, and Rhys stroked her thumb along Amy's jaw.

When they pulled apart Rhys lent down to clip Peggy's lead to her collar.

"It's been a long day. Thank you for waiting so we could go home together." Amy speaking broke the silence of the lobby. It nearly made Scarlet jump. She had to remind herself that, of course, Amy could speak out loud to someone when they weren't facing her. It just didn't work the other way around.

Rhys waited until she was standing up straight again before replying. She linked their fingers and pulled Amy's hand to her mouth. She looked into her eyes as she smiled and brushed her lips over the back of Amy's hand.

Scarlet stood near the top of the stairs for a long time after they left. The lobby was empty apart from a scattering of dried brown leaves that blew in throughout the day every time the automatic doors slid open. She slowly pressed her hand to her mouth, trying to hold in a sob.

Not her Rhys... Amy's Rhys? Rhys was with Amy?

She turned and sat down hard on the stairs. She stared off into the middle distance, her mind replaying all her past interactions with Rhys. She went over and over them, taking them apart piece by piece.

That first cup of coffee outside my tutor session.

Rhys giving me a special sign language nickname.

Rhys telling me about her Grandparents' holiday cottage.

How could I have been so stupid, so blind, so entitled to think Rhys would look at me twice?

Mum must have rubbed off on me. This is the same entitled way she pursues men. She never gives it a second thought that they might not be interested in her. She doesn't care that they might already be in a relationship. Of course they'd be interested!

I just thought it was serendipity that Rhys was the tutor of the sign language club. I was so happy to see her, I never thought to ask why she's so involved in the Deaf community. She mentioned doing sign interpreting in some other lectures. I just assumed it was part of her job. Now it makes sense; BSL is her girlfriend's first language.

The loud sound of a vacuum cleaner buzzing to life in the lobby jolted Scarlet back into awareness. She jerked upright and caught herself before she took a tumble down the stairs. Her whole body was stiff and her head swam. *How long have I been sitting here?*

She gripped the handrail and stumbled back down the stairs. Pulling her phone out of her pocket, she frantically checked the time. *Shit.*

The illuminated screen mocked her. 21:52.

500 words to go, eight minutes until the submission deadline.

It was an impossible task. She bolted from the bottom of the stairs back into the computer suite and almost skidded into her chair. Several heads shot up from the surrounding computers in alarm.

Come on, come on.

She frantically wiggled the mouse to wake up the login screen.

It took her three attempts to type in her username and password correctly.

21:55.

500 words short, five minutes to the submission deadline.

She hit 'Save As' and changed the filename to the assignment code and her student number. Next she navigated to the university website and found the assignment upload page.

21:58

500 words short, two minutes to the deadline. Tears streamed down her face as she hit the upload button. Her heart pounded as she watched the progress bar creep along the screen.

21:59

70% uploaded, then 80%, 90%. Scarlet hovered the mouse over the submit button, ready to click it as soon as the document was fully uploaded. Her hands trembled.

22:00

95%.

97%.

99%.

100%.

Click. Submit.

22:01

Did it go? Is it on there?

Was the deadline ten o'clock or by *ten o'clock?!*

Scarlet pried her stiff hand off of the mouse and wiped her sweaty palms on her trouser legs, then she used the sleeve of her hoodie to wipe the wet print of her hand off the mouse.

Her entire body ached from the tension she didn't realise she'd been holding until the adrenaline crashed out of her system.

She gathered her things and left.

Chapter Seventeen

The walk home was a void; Scarlet didn't remember any of it.

The warm air of the hallway woke her from autopilot as she entered the house from the freezing night outside. From down the hall, she could hear the sounds of her friends chatting and laughing in the kitchen. They called out to her when they heard the front door shut, but she ignored them and went straight up to her room.

She felt empty. All the energy had been sapped from her body once the adrenaline left her. She crawled into bed fully clothed, pulled the covers over her head, and cried.

The next morning Scarlet pressed a cold flannel to her puffy eyes, looked in disgust at her reflection in the mirror, and decided she wanted to go home. Marie might not be the most understanding and caring mother in the world, but at least she would have the comfort of her familiar childhood bedroom around her. Right now she craved peace and quiet to pull herself back together. University was too much, too stifling. She felt too raw to be around anyone.

Her friends had come upstairs and knocked on her door several times during the night, asking through the wood if she was okay. From her bed she called out that she was fine but didn't go to the door. It was hard knowing her friends were concerned about her, but she felt so embarrassed. She couldn't bring herself to tell them what was wrong.

What if she failed her course? She would lose her student finance and without that funding she wouldn't be able to pay her share of the rent.

What if she had to confess to her housemates she had to leave, that she had jeopardised their shared tenancy because of a stupid mistake? It wasn't fair to make them scramble to find a replacement housemate in the middle of the school year.

Guilt prickled her.

Falling for the head of your course? She gave herself a mental shake. Why had she done that? Forming attachments to inappropriate people— there was some psychology in that, something she hadn't studied yet.

At least Marie would leave her alone. She would have space to grieve her broken heart, space to work through her emotions. It wasn't fair for her to be grieving, Rhys had never been hers... and it was just one screwed up assignment.

She drove herself home, trying not to cry. She had fucked up badly, and she knew it.

Her mother's car wasn't on the driveway, and she breathed a sigh of relief at the temporary reprieve. *In terrible situations sometimes you have to find the small positives. A bit of extra time without mum is always a positive.*

She let herself in and went straight upstairs to the solace of her old bedroom and shut the door. Shutting out her problems for just a little bit longer wouldn't make them go away and definitely wouldn't make her feel any better in the long run, but there was comfort in the familiar.

Rhys was puzzled when Scarlet wasn't in her lecture on Thursday morning. She hoped the girl would open up to her during their planned chat afterwards. But she wasn't overly concerned. Scarlet probably came down with the Freshers' Flu — a cold that was sweeping the campus — and right now she was probably tucked up at home with a mug of Lemsip.

Each time she spoke to Scarlet outside of class, she got a sense that she was profoundly unhappy. She hoped it was just the change of coming to university and that Scarlet would find her stride soon.

Most students just needed a bit of time to settle into life away from home. Occasionally there would be a student who found it impossible to make the transition to student life, but they were the exception rather than the norm.

"What's the matter with you?" Marie pulled the covers off of her daughter. Scarlet turned away from her and curled into a foetal position.

"You didn't tell me you were coming, and it shocked me to see your car here last night. What if I'd brought Greg home for the evening?"

"Isn't this still my home too, mum?"

"Well—"

"Mum?" Scarlet said in a small voice.

"Well, you know, darling. You have a new home now; you moved out. You left me to live here on my own."

"That's not really how going away to university works."

"Well, it certainly feels that way to me. You've left me to sort all the bills on my own." Scarlett sat up in bed and turned to her mother. "And how have you been sorting those bills, mum? I think we really need to talk about this. I've been trying to talk about it for weeks."

"Don't turn this around on me, Scarlet. I'm your mother, you can stop treating me like I'm the child. I'm not stupid, you can stop treating me like I am—like you always do. You've always looked down on me."

"I don't look down on you, mum. I want you to be happy. I want you to understand you don't need the validation of a man for that. It doesn't have to be bought. You can make happiness for yourself."

"Oh, here we go again. Little miss high and mighty. You think you're so grown up and worldly because you're getting a university education. You, with your halloumi burgers and your waste of space girlfriends. You're into all this socialist rubbish; you know the statistics on how much greater a man's earning potential is compared to a woman's."

"I happen to like halloumi," Scarlet interjected in a small voice.

"You're shooting yourself in the foot with this lesbian thing. You could make so much more of yourself. But no, you've gone and fallen in love with a teacher!"

The reminder of her feelings for Rhys broke Scarlet. She had tried so hard to hold back the tears in front of her mother, but now she cried.

"Why are you here, anyway? Has she broken up with you already?"

"No," Scarlet mumbled.

"What was that?"

"I said no. There was never anything to break up. She wasn't interested in me like that."

"Oh, God, Scarlet, did she turn out to be straight? How could you have been so stupid? Well, at least that leaves you free to pursue more lucrative women."

"No, she — she's definitely gay. She's got a girl-friend." Scarlet's voice cracked on the last word, thinking back to seeing Rhys and Amy in the library.

"Is that all? For goodness' sake, Scarlet. Break them up if you're that infatuated with the woman, but you should be aiming higher!"

"No, mum. Just, no. I'm a good person."

I am *a good person.*

Chapter Eighteen

November ticked along as Scarlet spent the next two weeks hiding out at home. She avoided her mother as much as possible and dodged calls and texts from her housemates. The day after she arrived home she'd come down with a cold, and now she felt lethargic and groggy. Her bed had been her haven, and YouTube had been a welcome distraction from the real world. She knew she'd slept far too much and needed some fresh air.

She dragged herself into the shower, the hot water a welcome balm to her sore muscles and the steam worked wonders to clear her stuffy nose. After toweling off and making sure her hair was completely dry, Scarlet got ready to leave the house for the first time in weeks. When she returned from her quick walk to the corner shop, she plopped down at the kitchen table with a cup of tea. She felt exhausted from that short outing, but at least her head felt clearer.

It seemed that her mother had been avoiding her too as she'd been out of the house more often than not for the last two weeks. She was nowhere to be found now. Scarlet was glad for the peace and quiet. When her mother had been home, she made sure it was perfectly clear her daughter was an inconvenience, and her presence was getting in the way of Marie's plans. Greg had been over for dinner once, but the rest of the time Marie had been out, presumably at his house.

Scarlet pulled her iPad out of its case and opened her email app. For too long she had been avoiding her emails and messages, and now she felt anxiety creep over her as it had done over the last two weeks, but she couldn't put it off any longer. Her friends needed to know she was alive. She felt sick with herself, knowing she had surely worried them with her sudden disappearance. She had written a brief note to say she needed to go home for a few days, but a few days had come and gone with no update on when she would be back.

There was at least one message each day in their group chat, letting her know they were thinking of her. She didn't read back over the last two weeks of messages, but typed a quick reply letting them know she was sorry for the radio silence.

Telling them a small lie made her feel bad, but it allowed her to protect herself from the embarrassment of the truth. She told them her mother had been ill, and she'd gone home to look after her. She cringed at the lie, but she just couldn't tell them the truth. It would be too pathetic for them to find out she was pining after someone she had never had a chance with. Her mother had made sure that Scarlet was well aware of exactly how pathetic her situation was.

Lily replied almost instantly, wishing Scarlet's mum a speedy recovery and hoping that they would see Scarlet soon.

One hard task over with, Scarlet was soon hovering her finger over the email icon, a little red bubble next to it showed that she had 152 unread messages. She took a shaky breath and resolved herself to the task of clearing her inbox. Most of the emails were junk, and she was able to get the number down quickly. A few required her attention. She marked those as unread again to remind her to go back to them later. This was a tactic she often used, but unfortunately it sometimes meant messages slipped through. Messages she actually hadn't read yet could get mixed in with the ones she had, and on this occasion a new email popped into her inbox just as she closed the programme. The little red bubble changed from 5 to 6 unread emails unnoticed.

Scarlet didn't see the reminder email about her next piece of coursework which was due in the following day.

She put off taking responsibility for her absence; from uni in general, as well as absence from her friends. She filled her time finding tasks around the house that didn't really need doing. Some things they were paying Maggie to do and some things that could wait a few more weeks until she came home for the Christmas holidays. She finally realised what she was doing when she found herself on her hands and knees changing the filter on the washing machine.

Look at what you're doing, stop procrastinating! Do the chores that need to be done before going back to uni.

Now she had taken the first steps to get out of the hole she had made for herself, Scarlet spent the rest of the day actively preparing to return to uni. The washing machine hummed as she washed all of her clothes and then her bedding. It was windy and dry, so she took a risk and hung the washing out on the line, adding some extra pegs to make sure nothing blew away.

She used Marie's absence to have a good look around the whole house. It looked like her mother had been refusing to let Maggie clean her bedroom, Scarlet made a mental note to ask her mother about it after a brief look from the doorway. There were clothes draped across all available surfaces, and the bedside table had a collection of empty glasses on it.

The kitchen cupboards were full to bursting, a clear

sign that Marie had not been eating the food from the grocery shop that was being delivered each week. She was either eating out of the house for nearly every meal, or she was forsaking food for alcohol.

As her daughter, Scarlet knew that either was an entirely likely explanation.

Pulling some dry goods out of the cupboard, she filled a box. Briefly she noted the logo printed on the outside of the cardboard, it was one of Marie's favourite online shops. The box was heavy when she picked it up. Juggling it, she opened the door to take the overflow of food to Mrs Kent's house.

By the time she was back at her student house, laying on her bed, Scarlet had thoroughly convinced herself she was a bad friend, bad study partner, and a bad student. It didn't help that she'd missed at least four study sessions with her group and apart from a quick message to tell them she'd had to go home for a few days, she hadn't been in contact with them. She certainly hadn't been keeping up with the discussion in their group chat over the last few days. Still she put off getting in touch with them, sure that they would be angry with her. She couldn't face the confirmation of what a disappointment she was.

When she couldn't put it off any longer, she pulled

out her phone. Her heart raced with anxiety as she opened the messaging app.

The bottom dropped out of her stomach when she scanned the most recent messages in their chat. They had been discussing a 500 word case study analysis that had been due in the previous day.

No no no, not again. This can't be happening.

There definitely should've been an email reminder about the coursework. She switched to her email app and quickly found the unread automated message.

Not knowing whether to cry or scream, Scarlet balked. She had just begun to pull herself back together, and now this.

What a disaster this course was turning out to be.

If she hadn't started this course, she never would have met Rhys, never would have been so distracted and wouldn't have everything going wrong now.

While she stared at the screen, a new email appeared in her inbox. The sender's name was one she definitely didn't want to see.

To: Scarlet Robbins
<scarlet.robbins@dalesbury.ac.uk>
From: Rhys Hunter
<rhys.hunter@dalesbury.ac.uk>
Subject: Meeting with Department Head

Hello Scarlet,

I hope this finds you well.

I have scheduled a time for you to meet with me on Monday morning in my office to discuss your recent coursework and attendance.

9:00

Room 17-b

Psychology Faculty Building

Regards,

Dr Rhys Hunter BA, MA, PHD

Developmental Psychology Faculty Head

University of Dalesbury

The email from Rhys was so formal, Scarlet immediately began to over-analyse what that meant. She knew now her feelings for Rhys were unrequited, but she didn't think she had imagined the friendship developing between them. *Did I? Could I have been imagining that, too?*

Had she done something at their last meeting to offend Rhys? Perhaps she'd said something inappropriate? Her mind raced as she replayed the whole of their conversation, too caught up in the personal to remember the missed coursework.

Chapter Nineteen

The heating was turned up too high in the Psychology building. It rattled, a few years overdue for a replacement. Perhaps they'd find the money in next year's budget.

Rhys pushed her keyboard away in frustration, angry with herself for not getting to the bottom of whatever problem Scarlet was having before it affected her coursework. Why hadn't she pushed harder to get her student to confide in her about it? This was one of the worst parts of her job, having to call students in for a meeting about their work. It felt like a personal failing when someone on her course didn't do well because she prided herself on being approachable and hoped that her students felt they could come to her if they needed advice.

Rhys just hoped that it wasn't too late to provide

support to the girl she had begun to get to know this term.

It was late Friday afternoon and sending the meeting request to Scarlet had been the last thing for her to do. Amy had worked an early shift at the library and would be ready to go home at five o'clock. Rhys planned to take her girlfriend out to dinner tonight.

Normally they would take Peggy home first after a long day at the library with Amy. Peggy was such a hardworking little dog, and she was totally devoted to being Amy's ears and deserved an evening off. Normally, Peggy spent her off time snuggled up on Rhys' lap on the sofa.

Tonight they had an early reservation, and they wouldn't have time to take Peggy home first. It wasn't a problem, as Peggy would be happy to curl up by Amy's feet. They had been to the restaurant enough times before to know that the staff wouldn't distract the dog.

Then home for the weekend where Peggy could be properly off duty, and Rhys would have her girlfriend all to herself. And she meant to have her. Rhys was absolutely smitten with Amy, and she wanted to show her just how much. They'd both been busy this week, but now the weekend was here—no work, no students, no research projects. Just them.

Pushing the guilt around Scarlet's grades to one side, Rhys resolved to have a nice evening. Amy would be the perfect distraction from work this weekend. She would meet with Scarlet first thing on Monday morning, and there was nothing more she could do until then.

She took Amy out on Friday night for a meal in one of her favourite restaurants. They relaxed. No one asked to stroke Peggy, although a customer did ask the hostess why there was a dog somewhere that served food. The conversation took place behind Amy, so Rhys was able to keep it from her. She'd been ready to step in if needed, but the hostess had it all in hand and the person left in a huff after being told Peggy was an assistance dog and had every right to be there.

The rest of the weekend was perfect too.. Rhys went out for her morning run and woke Amy by slipping back into bed, naked and warm from the shower. They'd made love, gently at first, then with increasing passion as Amy became more fully awake. Later in the morning they agreed coffee and brunch were essential if they were going to do more than doze all day.

Amy caught her staring off into space while absent-mindedly stirring the scrambled eggs. Once she'd touched Rhys' arm to get her attention she hopped up onto the worktop next to the stove and signed "Are you ok?"

They usually spoke to each other in BSL at home. Rhys thought it was important to speak to Amy in her first language, rather than making her expel the mental energy she was constantly having to use in the hearing world.

Rhys hated to be distracted by thoughts of work when it was their weekend together, but the issues Scarlet was having were really bothering her. She loved being at home in their little bubble and didn't want to burden Amy with work stresses. It would also be a data breach to discuss a student with her girlfriend. Distraction was the best solution she could come up with for now, and Amy was alway a balm for her soul. Resolving to lose herself in their connection for the rest of the weekend, Rhys made the conscious decision to turn her full attention back to the moment.

"Yes, love, are you ok? I mean, you came so loudly earlier that Peg was howling along with you that last time."

"No, she wasn't! Peggy is a well-trained professional. It's her job to ignore distractions."

Rhys grinned, upping the banter between them. "You have no way of knowing for sure, you'll just have to trust me!"

"Oh, like I'm trusting you not to burn the eggs?"

Rhys took the pan off the heat and moved to stand between Amy's legs, her eyebrow raised in challenge. They both smiled into the kiss they shared. Rhys pulled her girlfriend's robe-clad body to the edge of the worktop and parted the material covering her bare skin.

Amy gasped at the intimate touch between her legs, of Rhys' fingers entering her, not for the first or even the second time that morning. Her sex was wet and ready, primed just by being near her lover in her half-dressed state, perpetually turned on by the love between them.

She threw back her head as Rhys kissed down her throat, along her collarbone and then further down to her breasts. Amy shuddered on the verge of orgasm when Rhys curled her fingers inside her, her thumb brushing against her clit with each thrust. Guessing what was about to happen, Rhys acted just in time, inserting her other hand behind Amy's head before it could slam back against the cabinet behind her. Having her girlfriend knock herself out was not the sort of oblivion she was aiming for.

Amy clung to her girlfriend while the waves of her orgasm calmed. Rhys made a discreet hand gesture to Peggy, telling her to howl. Then she caressed Amy's face, turning her chin gently so she could see what her very well-trained dog was doing. "See, love, you just don't know how loud you are!"

Amy's face slackened in shock until Rhys grinned and took pity on her, "I'm teasing you, babe. Good girl, Peg, you *are* very well trained."

Amy exclaimed through her laughter, "Ree, that's not funny! As punishment for being such an arsehole, you'll have to start the eggs from scratch again. I'll watch."

Chuckling, Rhys picked up the pan and tipped the rubbery yellow mess into the bin. Funnily enough, she didn't have any regrets about the wasted food.

"Amy, remind me again why you won't marry me?"

"Oh Ree, I'm sorry. I love you for your patience. I just. . ." Amy sighed, "You know how important my independence is to me." Rhys leaned over and kissed Amy softly, "I know."

"Hello Dr Hunter."

"Good morning." Rhys' smile didn't reach her eyes as she greeted Scarlet at her office door on Monday. She guided her to a chair and then perched herself on the edge of her desk.

Taking a deep breath, she cut right to the chase. "I'm sorry to tell you this, Scarlet, but you've failed module 108. You didn't meet the word count for your main essay, and we didn't receive a submission for the critical article analysis at all. We have some things to talk through; there are some options for you to think about. You can retake this module again next year, but you will only be able to achieve the basic pass mark as it will be a retake. That will also mean your workload will be more dense for a term."

Scarlet pinched the bridge of her nose and squeezed her eyes shut.

"What happened with your assignments, Scarlet?" Rhys sounded concerned. Her kindness made Scarlet feel angrier. *Why does my chest feel so tight?* For a second she didn't know if she was going to hyperventilate.

There was no clear direction for her burning frustration. *Should it be aimed at mum for monopolising my time and using up all of my mental energy? Rhys and Amy for being, well, Rhys and Amy? Or myself, for being so stupid?*

She couldn't hold her emotions in anymore and began to cry.

"Oh, Scarlet." Rhys scooted off the desk and knelt next to her, wrapping a comforting arm around her shoulders. Scarlet turned in the chair and flung herself into Rhys' arms. She sobbed into her neck, not caring that this was probably wildly inappropriate and not at all what Rhys had intended.

Her body didn't seem to get the message that this was a platonic touch and that she was angry with everything, including Rhys. Through the tightness in her chest, she felt her heart thud and her entire body felt hot. It felt like her heart was trying to beat with an enormous fist clenched around it. It hurt. It really, really hurt.

Everything was going so wrong.

She was in so much pain; she needed to lash out at something.

Something that her mother had said wormed its way into her mind. She gently pulled her phone out of her coat pocket, thankful that she had started keeping it on silent recently. Scarlet schooled her face into a blissed-out smile and discretely snapped a couple of photos of their embrace over Rhys' shoulder where the other woman couldn't see.

Chapter Twenty

The photos on her phone taunted Scarlet over the next few days. She stared at the screen, and her thumb swiped back and forth between the secret photos she'd snapped. Her mind went back and forth wondering what to do. She had been so angry and upset when she'd taken them; they felt like some kind of twisted insurance policy. Her mind bounced back and forth, like a devil and an angel sitting on her shoulders. The devil's voice was her mother and the angel was Amy.

Now she didn't know whether she had been angry and upset with Rhys, the situation, or more likely herself. She knew it was wrong to take the photos behind Rhys' back, but she kept hearing the disappointment in her mother's voice and the accusations her mother levied against her.

Mum's insistent that I take care of us both now I'm an adult. She doesn't care what's best for my mental health; her only concern is for what makes her life more comfortable. She doesn't really believe in mental health. She's always thought me doing a psychology degree was a waste of time. She certainly isn't shy about letting me know her opinions on the matter. Mum has always wanted me to achieve status in life. It's like she thinks she's failed in her duty as a mother if she doesn't groom me to marry up.

She looked at the photos again. Her own face was clear, and she really could've been hugging anyone if it weren't for the distinctive tattoo showing below the rolled-up sleeve of Rhys' shirt.

For better or worse, Scarlet closed the photo app without deleting the pictures.

On Wednesdays Amy took Peggy to an assistance dog training class. The evenings were dark now, but she didn't mind the long drive because it gave Peggy a chance to be with other dogs with the same responsibilities.

It was also important to Amy that she go to these sessions. She was mentoring some members of the group with their new dogs, and she always had a good time in their company. It wasn't just a training class, but also an important social event. Some of the members of the group lived too far out from Dalesbury to benefit from the town's Deaf Community. For a couple of people here tonight, it was their only chance to talk to other people who signed.

They always took a long break halfway through the class. Cups of tea and coffee were passed around, and the dogs were given the "Off Duty" command to play in the middle of the hall while their humans shared out cake.

"Mmm, this lemon cake is so nice, Anne!" Amy signed to an older woman who blushed and signed her thanks.

"Would you like another piece, Amy?"

Amy shook her head. "I'm meeting Rhys at her parent's house for dinner."

"How is that hunky woman of yours? We haven't seen her for a while," Betty leaned over to ask. "And more importantly, what's her dad cooking for dinner this week?"

The group laughed while Betty protested, "What? I mostly eat frozen meals for one these days. I have to live vicariously through you young people."

Amy smiled, "You know I don't often bring Rhys. Peggy and I value our independence too much."

The second half of the session was filled with as much laughter as the break. Peggy was just as unhappy to leave her doggy friends as Amy was to leave her human ones. *I know I'm lucky to have Rhys; we never have any problems communicating. Some of my friends will go home to empty houses or families they can't understand.*

The car warmed up nicely as they headed towards home. The rain beat against the windscreen. The wipers swished back and forth, trying to keep up with clearing the raindrops. Peggy listened to the wind howling as she sat on the front passenger seat with her car harness clipped into the seatbelt.

Tonight Marie was alone. Greg was with his kids, so she was bored. If that stupid boy hadn't broken his arm she would have Greg with her. Her empty glass thudded down onto the table, and she realised the bottle on the worktop was also empty. The glass tottered on the table-top, and before it came to rest, Marie picked up her bag and shrugged her coat on. She staggered down the hall-way, grabbing her car keys as she passed the sideboard by the door. There was still a spattering of rain as she left the house and slid into the driver's seat. She was already driving along the main road before her brain caught up and tried to decide where she was going. She could either go to the shop and buy a new bottle of vodka or she could head somewhere more sociable to get a drink. The street lights were bright along the road and Marie didn't notice the oncoming cars flashing their headlights at her, trying to warn her that she hadn't switched her own headlights on.

She was thinking about where to go to find her next drink when she pulled onto the slip road.

The crash startled Amy.

Something hit her as she was going along the motorway. The whole car jolted and its back end tried to swerve to the side. Peggy was thrown forward, but she was saved from hitting the dash by her car restraint harness.

Luckily, Amy hadn't been driving fast because of the wet weather. Braking gently, she pulled onto the hard shoulder. A shudder went through her. She looked around and still couldn't immediately see what had collided with her car. It was so wet and dark. Other cars' headlights sparkled off the raindrops on her windscreen, making her squint into the gloom. Each one that passed sent a wave of vibration rocking through her car. Eventually she could make out the dark shape of another car, stopped at the side of the road. Its lights were out, and she couldn't tell whether the crumpled front bumper was the cause for the car not having any lights. *Had the car had its headlights on?* She was sure she hadn't seen any headlights or tail lights coming along the slip road to the side of her.

Her hands shook when she went to pry them off the steering wheel; she'd been holding the wheel so tightly that her fingers had cramped. Tears trickled from the corners of her eyes, and she put out her sore hand to check on Peggy.

Peggy whined, and Amy could feel the vibration of it through her fur. She touched her dog gingerly, trying to work out whether she was hurt. She was so scared that something might have happened to Peggy; she didn't like to think how she would cope without her. She reassured herself that Peggy was probably just a little bit bruised where the chest plate of the harness had caught her. She was a well-trained dog, used to staying calm in unexpected situations.

"Good girl, Pegs," Amy whispered, just loud enough to be heard above the rain. "You're such a good girl." She stroked Peggy's head, calming herself as much as her dog.

The side of the road was dark, with only the occasional set of car headlights passing through the darkness. Amy knew she should get out of the car as soon as possible because there was always a danger of other traffic hitting them where they sat on the hard shoulder.

She also needed to check on the occupants of the other car. She could make out now that it was an Audi and there appeared to be a woman in the driver's seat. There could be other people in the car too, people Amy couldn't see, perhaps even children in the back seat. Her fear for them made her move. Amy unclipped Peggy's harness and readied herself to get out of her car. She put her hazards on, but she wasn't sure if the rear lights were working after the damage from the crash . *We need to be as visible as possible to the cars coming down the road behind us.*

Peggy alerted to a noise just as Amy felt a different set of vibrations through the car. These were sharper and quicker. It took her a few seconds to recognise them as someone knocking against glass. Turning, she saw a woman in the rain next to the passenger window. Her mouth was moving, and she was insistently knocking on the glass. It was too dark for her to properly make out the shapes that the woman's lips were making. She tried to turn on the interior light to see better. Her hands were shaking so badly it took a while to find the switch. The interior light didn't help much; it just added to the reflections on the glass and the raindrops.

The woman, who must have been the driver from the other car, yanked open the passenger door, startling Peggy. Amy could see she was in a full on rant, leaning over the top of the terrier to shout at Amy. Amy's heart beat hard, and she tried not to panic. It was important she keep calm and try to calm this other woman down. She also knew they needed to move away from the road and the precarious position their cars had been forced to stop in. The feeling of responsibility to make sure they were all safe weighed on her.

Amy tried to tell the stranger they needed to get away from the cars, to get to a safe place further up the grass verge at the side of the road. But the woman talked over Amy. She couldn't always regulate the volume of her own voice. *Perhaps I'm not talking loudly enough? Or perhaps she's ignoring me on purpose?*

Amy couldn't make out what she was saying. The light wasn't really good enough to lipread clearly, and it almost seemed like her words were running into one another. Amy shook her head trying to clear it. She didn't think she'd hit her head on anything. Her airbags hadn't deployed. Why couldn't she focus properly on the woman's lips?

She tried to tell her she was deaf and couldn't hear what she was saying. This just seemed to make the angry woman rant even more. Frustrated, Amy held up a hand and said loudly, "Stop. I can't understand what you're saying. It's too dark for me to lipread as quickly as normal. Please slow down."

Marie was disgusted. *That disabled girl has wrecked my car, and she's more concerned about a stupid dog than trying to sort out the problem.* Marie had gone over to the other car to demand to know why the other driver had swerved into her as she pulled off of the slip road. The rain soaked her jacket, and it plastered her hair to her head. They'd both stood at the side of the road, and the girl tried to get her to do something with her phone, but Marie wasn't having any of that. That ratty dog had been walking in circles around its owner, distracting Marie with its wet little body.

She was no closer to getting the girl's contact details. She would get her to pay for all the damage one way or another.

There was no choice, she had to convince the girl to pay privately. In the few minutes straight after the crash, Marie remembered the monthly payment for her car insurance bounced a few weeks ago. If the girl insisted on going through the insurance company, then she would be in big trouble. It simply couldn't be allowed to happen, no matter what she had to do.

Rhys had just arrived at her parents' house when her phone rang with its FaceTime tone. Both she and Amy would normally meet there for a midweek dinner after Amy's training session with Peggy. The smell of her dad's chicken stir-fry wafted down the hallway as she fished her phone out of her pocket. "Hey, babe."

"Rhys!" Amy was almost concealed in darkness, her hood pulled up over her head to keep out the worst of the rain. It looked like she held something in her spare hand to shield the phone from getting soaked too. When a passing car's headlights briefly lit up Amy's face, Rhys could see that it was the big UK street atlas that Amy's dad insisted they all carry in their cars.

The sudden flash of light also made her aware of the tears streaming down her girlfriend's cheeks. Her bottom lip trembled on the tiny phone screen.

"Ree, the car's smashed up. . . can you come?" *She's scared.* Rhys knew it took a lot for Amy to admit that she needed help. "Of course. Are you hurt?"

"No."

Rhys sighed with relief. "Is Peggy hurt?"

"I don't think so; I felt her as best I could. Ree, I don't know how far along the road I am."

"Don't worry, I can find your phone's GPS. Are you somewhere safe? Are you away from the road?"

"Yes, Peggy and I are up the grass verge under a tree."

"Good. I'm at mum and dad's house so I'll be there in about 20 minutes. I love you."

"I love you too. Should I text the breakdown service?"

"It'll take them ages to come out. Let's see if we can tow it first."

While they'd been talking, Rhys' parents, Kevin and Helen, came to see what was going on. By the time Rhys assured herself Amy was safe and was ready to head back out to her own car, Kevin was pulling his coat on too and her mother was pressing a big thermos flask of tea into her hands with a worried look on her face.

"Come on, kid; let's go get your girl." Despite the situation, Rhys shook her head at her dad. She was approaching forty, but he would always insist on calling her "kid". Helen had produced several big towels out of thin air, and now Rhys was trying to balance them and the flask in her arms while getting into her dad's Jeep.

———

Amy was just beginning to panic when Kevin's Jeep pulled up in front of her car. The woman from the Audi had gone and sat back in her own car, refusing to listen to Amy's warnings of how dangerous it was to be in a car parked on the hard shoulder. Every time a vehicle passed, their cars shook and Amy was terrified that something would hit them in the dark.

By the time Rhys rushed up the bank towards her, she was shaking and on the verge of hyperventilating.

Amy clung to her girlfriend desperately. It was too dark to see properly, but Rhys unzipped her own coat and pulled Amy into its warmth with her. She took Amy's hand, pulled its glove off and pressed her fingers to her mouth, letting Amy read her lips by touch instead of sight.

"I'm here, dad's looking at your car. What do you need me to do?"

Amy's face pressed into Rhys' neck. She wanted to block everything out, but she couldn't get her breathing back to normal.

"Can't. Breathe." She rubbed at her throat until Rhys took her hand again and put it back on her own mouth.

"Okay, it's a panic attack. I've got you. I know it feels horrendous, but it will pass."

She guided Amy's cheek to her chest. "Feel my heartbeat. Can you concentrate on that?"

Amy closed her eyes, blocking out the rain and flashes of headlights. She felt the thud-thud of Rhys' heart vibrating through her breastbone. She pressed her cheek tighter to her girlfriend's skin. Slowly but surely, her own heart slowed to a calmer rhythm.

Chapter Twenty-One

Once Amy's breathing slowed and she could talk normally, Rhys asked again, "What would you like me to do?"

"Can you speak to the lady in the other car? It was too dark for me to see what she was saying. She was talking too quickly, I couldn't read her lips. I tried to get her to type what she was saying on my phone, but she stormed off. I told her it was dangerous to sit in a car on the hard shoulder with the traffic moving right next to it, but she didn't pay any attention." *She said I shouldn't be driving.*

"Ok, I'll talk to her. But first, can you tell me what happened?"

"I don't know what happened. I was driving slowly because of the rain, then I felt the crash. I pulled the car over, then I realised there was another car pulled up behind me."

"You didn't see the other car until after you pulled over? She must have come along the slip road and hit you because all the damage is on your passenger side and her front end's smashed up."

"No, I... it was dark, I didn't see her." Amy wiped water from her face. Her hands began to shake again. "Why didn't I see her?"

"Perhaps she had a headlight out. You're a good driver, Amy. This wasn't your fault." Rhys glanced over to where her dad was attaching the tow rope to the front of Amy's car. She waved at him, and he retrieved a towel and the flask of tea from the Jeep before he jogged up the verge to meet them.

Amy soon found herself and Peggy wrapped in the fluffy towel and a mug of tea in her trembling hands. Kevin sat down opposite her under the tree, placing a camping lantern on the ground which shone a comforting light in a three-foot radius around them.

Amy gripped Rhys' fingers for as long as she could before reluctantly letting go. She knew Rhys needed to go talk to the lady in the Audi so they could all get on their way, but fear gripped her with the thought a lorry would hit their prone cars.

"It's okay, love. I'll be quick. I'll get her contact details, and then we'll get you home."

Amy flinched as a van sped passed them along the

road. Then she nodded up at Rhys with tears in her eyes. Kevin reached over and gently put his hand on top of Amy's as Rhys carefully made her way down the slippery verge to the damaged cars.

"I'm sorry to drag you out in this horrible weather, Kevin. I should've been able to deal with this myself, I feel so useless." She motioned to the side of her head then hugged her knees against her chest.

"You're not useless, sweetheart. It's just because of the rain and the darkness. Any other day you could have dealt with all of this yourself. I know that, and Rhys knows that. Now you need to believe it, too."

Amy smiled wanly at Kevin in the dim light, which was just bright enough to read his lips. *I hate feeling like a damsel in distress.*

Marie helped herself to her fourth polo mint. It was the only edible thing she could find in her handbag. She had phoned Greg, and now it was just a waiting game to see how quickly he got to her. She told him she'd called her insurance company's breakdown service, but the young girl in the call centre had been completely incompetent and couldn't organise a tow quickly enough. Her entire body felt heavy, and she thought she might be sick as she realised that she might have actually got herself into real trouble this time. She needed to make sure she managed this situation carefully. The other driver must not, under any circumstances, call the police or involve their insurance companies.

Through the raindrops on the window, she could see one of the people who'd come to tow the disabled girl's car walking down the verge.

She groaned when her passenger door was pulled open and a new woman with short dark hair ducked her head into the car. "Hello, are you hurt?"

Marie squeezed her eyes shut for a second and shook her head to clear the fuzzy feeling. She still felt sick. Panic rose in her chest as she searched for the right words. *Never admit fault, never admit fault.*

She gripped her neck where it met her shoulder and winced. *Whiplash was a common thing, wasn't it?* "I'm definitely going to be sore tomorrow, that's for sure."

"Can you walk? We really need to get away from the side of the road."

"I'm fine where I am, thank you very much."

"Well, really the advice is to get out of your vehicle as soon as possible and get a safe distance away from the roadside."

"It's raining." Marie deadpanned, staring at the stranger as if it was the most solid argument in the world. She knew she needed to get rid of this woman as quickly as possible. The sooner she could get them to tow the other car away, the less chance the police would be called and want her to do a breathalyser test.

"It's just water; better to be a bit wet than sitting in the car if something else hits you from behind."

"That's not going to happen. Just give me your contact details, and we can sort this out tomorrow. We can sort it out amongst ourselves."

Rhys pulled out her phone, using the car doorway to shield it from the rain. She opened her Notes app. "What's your name?"

She typed in Marie's answers as they spoke.

"And your phone number? Your registration number? And who is your insurance with?"

"Look, just leave me in peace and phone me tomorrow. That girl obviously shouldn't be driving. She's disabled; it's not right. Does the government even know she's driving?"

"Just hold on a minute; I don't appreciate you speaking about Amy that way. She is an excellent driver. You don't have any reason to think her deafness contributed to the crash."

"Well, perhaps she was paying more attention to that animal than she was to the road. It should be locked in the boot."

"You are talking about a highly trained assistance dog, a living, breathing piece of medical equipment." The woman's tone had upset her, "You know what, fine. If you can't talk reasonably, I'll phone you tomorrow."

Rhys didn't mean to close the woman's car door quite as hard as she did. It slammed loudly. She liked to think it was partly because of the stormy weather and not solely down to the anger she felt on Amy's behalf.

She took a quick photo of the front of the Audi and the side of Amy's car, then stood further up the verge to get a picture of the two cars together. Amy, Kevin, and Peggy came out from under the tree, ready to tow Amy's car away.

They got Peggy into the backseat and wrapped a fresh towel around her. She curled up and burrowed her head into her cocoon. Amy climbed up into the passenger seat with another towel around her shoulders while Rhys got behind the steering wheel. Kevin got into Amy's car to steer it while it was being pulled along behind the Jeep.

Amy was shivering next to Rhys as they drove back to her parents' house. Her hands clasped tightly in her lap, the knuckles white. Rhys gently eased one hand into her own and put Amy's fingers against her lips. "I love you Amy. You're safe."

Chapter Twenty-Two

That night Amy woke up gasping for breath. The room was dark apart from the moonlight shining in around the edges of the curtains. *Why is the window over there? It's okay, we're in Kevin and Helen's spare room. They insisted we stay overnight.*

Peggy felt Amy sit up and wiggled her way up from the foot of the bed and into Amy's arms. Amy pressed her face into her dog's fur and began to cry quietly. Peggy whined, feeling her owner's sadness. Soon Rhys' arms wrapped around both woman and dog, pulling them into her warmth.

They didn't speak; no words were needed. They just held each other until Amy's heartbeat and breathing calmed down. Rhys kissed the top of her girlfriend's head, and Amy lifted her chin for a kiss on the lips.

Peggy tilted her head to the side and contemplated them for a moment before jumping down from the bed and curling up in her basket on the other side of the room. Amy felt Rhys chuckle and put her fingers to her lips in time to feel her say, "Oh Peg, you don't have to go, we're not about to—"

"Aren't we?" Amy whispered, slipping a leg over Rhys' thighs to straddle her lap. Rhys' hands automatically went to her girlfriend's hips, her fingertips gently caressing the skin exposed between pyjama top and bottoms. When they arrived back the night before, Rhys' mum produced the sleepwear she'd intended to give them for Christmas. *Thank goodness Helen's an early bird when it comes to Christmas presents.*

"I need you to distract me. Please, Ree? I need to be reminded that we're all okay, that I'm okay. That we're alive, and safe, and connected, and we love each other."

"That dog is very finely attuned to your needs, isn't she?"

"Shhhhh." She rocked her hips deliberately against Rhys' lap, and pressed her fingers harder on her mouth to muffle the groan she felt vibrate up from her girlfriend's throat.

Soon Amy found herself pressed to the bed on her back. She lifted her hips to help Rhys wiggle her out of her pyjama bottoms.

Kissing her way down Amy's stomach, Rhys smiled as she felt the muscles flutter beneath the skin in anticipation of where her mouth would travel next. Amy parted her legs in encouragement and shuddered as she felt Rhys' breath on her centre. Nothing could simultaneously ground her and take her away from it all quite like this intimacy with her girlfriend.

Gasping, Amy quickly covered her mouth with her arm as Rhys' tongue took up a familiar rhythm against her clit. She squirmed and pressed her hips up toward Rhys' mouth. Over and over again, they moved together, until Amy tensed with the wave of orgasm rolling through her. Her head swam, and only after her vision cleared did she realise she'd left teeth marks on her own forearm.

Amy tasted herself on Rhys' lips as they kissed. She was still on her back, and Rhys used her arms to brace her weight over her. Sliding her hands down Rhys' back, Amy pushed her way under the material covering her girlfriend's backside, and squeezed. While they kissed, one of Amy's hands found its way between their bodies and pressed against Rhys through her pyjama bottoms.

Rhys lifted onto her knees to give Amy more room to get her hand under the material. She gasped into Amy's mouth when her fingers slid through the wet heat between her legs. It wasn't easy to be quiet with Amy touching her so expertly; she would normally moan and cry out her pleasure. Amy could feel the vibrations from the sounds she made when they made love. But here, in her parents' house, she had to be more considerate. She wasn't a teenager anymore; she had more control of herself. She had more maturity than to wake up her parents with sounds of sex coming from her bedroom. She controlled her breathing and listened long enough to reassure herself the bed wasn't squeaking under their movement. Happy they were being quiet enough, she relaxed into the rhythm that Amy set, her orgasm fast approaching.

Kevin and Helen had long since cleared away the breakfast things when Rhys and Amy came downstairs the next morning.

"Did you sleep okay, girls?" Kevin asked, looking up from where he was reading the newspaper on his iPad.

"Eventually, dad."

"That's good. Let's get some breakfast inside you, then everything will look better. Cereal? Toast?" He stood and passed around bowls and spoons. "We've got cornflakes, muesli or shredded wheat. I can slice some banana to go on top if you like."

"Sounds great." Amy said, but she didn't manage to inject her voice with enthusiasm. Kevin was a feeder who loved problem solving with food. He'd soon set them up with their choice of cereal. Then he ducked out of the kitchen to look at the damage to Amy's car in the daylight.

Amy ate slowly, chewing each mouthful carefully. No matter how thoroughly she chewed; it still felt like swallowing rocks. She persevered, knowing she barely managed any of her dinner the night before. Rhys finished long before Amy got to her last spoonful. She waited for Amy to finish before taking both of their bowls to the dishwasher.

Kevin came in through the back door and started talking to Rhys. Amy looked at them in profile, back-lit by the late morning sunlight pouring in from the window behind them. She turned back to the table where Helen was still sitting next to her and asked, "Are they talking about my car?"

"Yes, dear." Helen took her hand and squeezed as Rhys and Kevin sat back at the table.

Rhys said, "I know everything is still very fresh. Do you want to talk about it now or—"

"I'm okay. I think it would be better to get it all sorted out as quickly as possible and then put it behind us."

"Okay. I have the lady's details. I'll call the insurance company and get the ball rolling."

"She said 'no insurance companies.' She said she would have my driving license taken away from me!" Amy's voice was panicked, her eyes wide and pleading with Rhys.

Helen asked, "Can she do that?" as she put fresh

coffee down in front of them. Rhys shook her head at her mum.

"I don't think so." She turned back to Amy and took her hand, "I thought you said you didn't speak to her?"

"I caught a few words. Important ones, you know, like 'dangerous', 'disabled', and 'shouldn't be driving'."

"Love, why didn't you say anything last night?"

"I didn't want you to go into the conversation angry with her. I can't lose my driving license, Ree, I just can't. I'd lose my independence."

"I know, love, I know. Don't worry, there's no reason for her to claim you shouldn't be driving. You haven't done anything wrong. She was very keen to sort this out without involving the insurance companies. It makes me suspicious when someone says that. There must be a reason she was so keen to sort it out privately."

"Maybe she's recently claimed and can't afford for her premiums to go up any more?" Helen asked optimistically.

"Oh, mum, you always see the best in people, and I love you for that," Rhys said. "But there was definitely something off about her. Babe," she addressed Amy, "You said you couldn't make out what she was saying properly? I know it was dark, but was she slurring her words?"

Kevin frowned and asked, "What are you suggesting, kiddo?"

"Well, she smelt very strongly of mints when I spoke

to her in her car. Perhaps she was trying to cover the smell of alcohol?"

"I couldn't see her properly, but it was like her words were running together. It made me think I might've hit my head. I couldn't work out why I couldn't see what she was saying."

"I don't think it was you. I think she might have been drunk. If we inform the police now, it'll be too late for them to do a breathalyser on her, but we can still tell her insurance company."

"No, Ree, listen, I'm scared they'll take my license away. I, I don't think I could cope if they took my independence away. Let's not risk it; we should just let it go."

"I promise that's not going to happen, Amy."

"But sometimes things go wrong. Paperwork gets lost. People who've never met you make stupid decisions without realising the effect they're having on your life. It happens all the time! She told me she'd have my driving license taken away from me. What if she really can do it? I don't want to chance it!"

Amy's voice rose more and more as she begged Rhys. *Please listen to me. Hear what I'm saying. You're normally so good at that.*

Chapter Twenty-Three

S carlet was taking great care to act as normally as possible, socialising with her housemates and meeting up with her study group. She ploughed along with her coursework, her head steadfastly buried in the sand about how close she was to being in real trouble with the university. There was only a very thin thread holding her together. She didn't attempt to contact her mother, and in turn, her mother hadn't tried to contact her.

It had been a week since her meeting with Dr Hunter. She'd played it back in her mind over and over. Sometimes she acted differently in the meeting. In her mind she had screamed at Rhys that it was all her fault — she had led Scarlet on, made her think there was a chance they could be together. Or sometimes she told Rhys her mother was ill and begged for special circumstances to be applied to her grade. She came up with so many excuses she could've offered Rhys, but deep down she knew her own mind had been playing tricks on her. She was still angry. Angry with Rhys, angry with herself, and angry with her mother.

She was ashamed of herself, because she still wanted Rhys. She felt the same longing when she thought about her, and she knew it was wrong. Rhys was Amy's girlfriend.

Oh God, did I miss a wedding ring? Could they be married? I can't be that person, desperately going after married women.

At least I'd be my mother's daughter. She shuddered at the thought.

As if conjured by Scarlet thinking of her, her mother's face lit up her phone screen. Surprised, she couldn't stop the second of hope that warmed her chest with thoughts her mum actually wanted to speak to her. That feeling never lasted long, but she hadn't managed to train herself out of feeling it.

"Scarlet, darling," Marie's voice boomed through the tiny phone speaker, "What are you up to?"

"Why are you shouting, mum?"

"Am I, darling? I didn't realise. I'm borrowing Greg's car, and you're coming through the Bluetooth thing. Are you sure you can hear me?"

"Yes, mum." Scarlet fought not to roll her eyes, then

remembered her mum couldn't see her and rolled them anyway. "Why are you driving Greg's car?"

"Oh, don't worry, darling. My car's just had to go to the garage for a little tidy up. Nothing major. Greg's helping me sort it out."

"Do you mean Greg is paying for it, mum?"

"Well, yes, I guess you could say it like that, darling, if you want to be crude."

Scarlet shook her head. "How can I help, mum?"

Why are you phoning me?

"Can't a mother just phone her daughter for a chat, darling?"

Not you, mother.

"I was just wondering, darling?"

Oh, here we go. Scarlet thought.

"How are you getting on with your little project?"

Scarlet wrinkled her brows in confusion, even though her mum couldn't see it. *Does mum somehow know about my grades? About my failings? How could she know, has the uni written to my home address? Play it cool.*

"What project are you talking about, mum?"

"Why, your little student/teacher fling, of course, darling," Scarlet almost sighed with relief before her mother's words registered, and she gave a spluttering cough.

"Mother! It's not a fling; it's not anything at all! Dr

Hunter has a girlfriend. She's a really nice lady; she works in the library on campus. She has a hearing dog called Peggy, who is just the sweetest and most hardworking little thing. It's amazing how Peggy helps Amy—"

Marie had started to tune out her daughter as she drove. She didn't care about Scarlet's schoolgirl crush, and she definitely wasn't interested in hearing about some teacher's girlfriend and her dog. *Wait, did I hear that right? The girlfriend has a hearing dog called Peggy? Wasn't that the name the stupid disabled girl had called her dog after the crash?* Marie realised suddenly that she'd already met Scarlet's fabled Dr Hunter. She must have been the woman who showed up after the crash to rescue the deaf girl.

"So, Scarlet, darling, tell me; what are you going to do about it?"

"What do you mean, mum?"

"Well, you want her, don't you, darling? Your Dr Hunter?"

"She's not 'my' anything mum. She never was." Scarlet tried hard to keep the dejection from her voice, but she wasn't sure she did a very good job of it.

"Oh come on now, darling, buck up. If you want her, why shouldn't you have her? Does she think she's too good for you?"

"Honestly, mum, she only ever saw me as one of her students. I know now she's in a serious relationship."

"Relationships come and go, darling. That's why you should wring them for all they're worth." Scarlet wasn't sure whether her mother was talking about the relationship or the person themselves. It wasn't Marie's usual MO to leave her man with nothing. She wasn't a con artist who bled men dry. She just sucked as much as she could out of the relationship without crossing the line into illegal activities.

"She's just a lecturer, mum. She's not loaded, I can't wring any money out of her."

Marie's eyes lit up as a plan formed in her mind. *But we could wring it out of the university. And if it ruined that teacher's reputation in the process? So what? She shouldn't have spoken to me like that after the crash.*

"Sex." Marie blurted into the phone.

"What?! What did you say, mum?"

"That's what you wanted from her, correct? If it wasn't money and it wasn't for her to fix your grades, then it must have been sex."

Marie's words startled Scarlet. *Fix my grades? Perhaps mum does know about me failing Rhys' class.* Scarlet's mind started turning in circles. *Perhaps I can convince Rhys to fix this mistake for me? Appealing to her as a student didn't work, but maybe mum's right, maybe Rhys can be tempted. If I use my feminine wiles on her, perhaps she'll amend my grade. That's just a pipe dream though, isn't it?*

She pushed the obvious objectification by her mother aside as the thought began to take root. She briefly wondered why Marie was encouraging her to pursue a relationship with Rhys now, when she'd thought it was such a terrible idea a few weeks ago. The thought was brief though, and Scarlet quickly forgot about it as she began fantasising about how she could kill two birds with one stone. Get Rhys and get her grades back on track. Deep inside she knew it was wrong, but she was desperate to salvage her place at university. She couldn't allow herself to become a failure at that, too.

Marie smiled to herself after she hung up with her daughter. This was better than she could have imagined. This situation could be used to her advantage. What luck that the people she'd had a run in with were the very people Scarlet was so upset with too.

How dare that Dr Hunter pass over her daughter for the disabled girl? What a miserable life they must have. *Well, surely it won't be too hard for Scarlet to get between them, what could that lecturer see in the deaf girl anyway? It must just be pity that's keeping them together. But if Scarlet can get in with her dear teacher, then I can press the university with legal action. One of their esteemed staff taking advantage of a student! I'm sure they'll offer a nice payout to keep that quiet!*

All Marie needed to do was coach her daughter into getting involved with the woman, then collect some evidence of their relationship. Yes, the big-wigs at the university would pay whatever she wanted to keep the scandal quiet. Her heart raced as she thought about the payout something like that could get her. And, of course, she would be there to comfort her poor naïve daughter after she'd been taken advantage of.

She chuckled in glee at the thought, nearly clipping the wing mirror of Greg's car on a parked van in her distraction.

The sign for the shopping centre's massive car park appeared, and she turned in, her insides fluttering in anticipation of the spending spree she was about to go on with Greg's credit card. She deserved some nice new things after the trauma of the car crash.

Chapter Twenty-Four

The following Thursday Scarlet returned to BSL class. She hadn't been back since the week before she found out about Rhys and Amy. It was hard enough seeing Rhys in her professional role as her lecturer, but the class was informal and reminded her too much of the personal relationship she'd thought was developing between them. She had also been steadfastly avoiding the library, not wanting to see Amy either.

To return to BSL class, she had to psych herself up to seeing Rhys in such close quarters again, but if she wanted to follow through with her mother's plan she needed to act like everything was fine around Rhys. It was no accident that she didn't arrive at the class early like she had before; she didn't want her first interaction with Rhys to be an awkward solo encounter when the last time she'd seen her had been when she'd cried on her shoulder.

As Scarlet walked down the corridor, she sighed in relief when she heard several voices coming from the classroom. Luckily, she had succeeded in not being the first one there. She wrapped her scarf around her neck several times to create a safety barrier between her and the rest of the world, then ducked into the room. About a third of the class were already there, and she carefully chose her chair so she was neither right next to nor opposite Rhys.

I need to have some gentle reacquainting interactions with her before I can press for more.

The room was chilly. The high ceilings and ill-fitting sash windows made it difficult to heat the building effectively. But Creasy Hall was a quirky part of the university campus. It made the students feel like they were attending a prestigious old college because some of the buildings had such interesting history. Scarlet watched the windows rattle in their frames as the last few class members took their seats.

Even still wrapped up in her coat, Rhys looked as attractive as ever.. Scarlet's heart ached to see her. She looked cold, and Scarlet wanted nothing more than to chafe Rhys' chilly fingers between her own warm ones. Rhys blew into her hands and rubbed them together to generate some heat so she could separate the pages of the handouts she was going to give out.

When she got to Scarlet, she paused with a smile, glad to see her integrating herself back into university life again.

"It's good to see you, Scarlet. I'm glad you've made it back to class. I think this could be something really great for you."

Scarlet felt her face heating just from being this close to the victim of her affection. She smiled shyly and adjusted the scarf around her face with one hand. The other reached for the handouts Rhys held out to her. She accidentally-on-purpose let her fingers brush Rhys' as she took the papers and flinched when she felt how cold they really were. "Are you okay? You're freezing."

"I'm fine, just coming down with a bit of a cold, I think. I got caught out in the rain a few nights ago. Nothing a bit of Lemsip won't fix." She tucked the remaining papers under her arm so she could rub her hands together again before continuing around the circle to give the other students their copies.

Scarlet kicked herself for not striking up more of a conversation. *How am I ever going to alter the way Rhys sees me if I can't be anything more than a blushing student in front of her?* She busied herself with looking over this week's handouts — Jobs. The sheets listed some different jobs that people might do: nurse, doctor, teacher, bus driver.

Rhys returned to her empty chair in the circle and began by recapping what they'd covered the previous week with a quick promise to give out those handouts to the students who had missed that session at the end of the class.

They learnt how to ask someone what their job was and practiced the ones on the sheet. Then, like before, Rhys paired them up and gave them all some flash cards with jobs listed on them, then the students took turns asking and replying to each other. For a while Scarlet forgot about life outside of the little cold classroom and just enjoyed herself. *I really do have an aptitude for learning this, just like Rhys said.*

After some warm-up interactions during the class, her plan was to wait around at the end like last time to get some one-on-one time with Rhys. She was hoping to entice her into going for an actual real-life evening drink, and so she had dressed up, knowing she would probably keep her coat on in the cold classroom. As they reached the halfway point of the class, Scarlet decided it was time to get Rhys to notice her a bit more, so she slipped off her coat to reveal the tight jeans and scoop neck top she was wearing underneath. She waited until she saw Rhys' eyes flit to her and then let her handouts slip off her lap and onto the floor. She made sure she had Rhys' full attention before deliberately bending forward to retrieve the slippery papers.

On her way back up she plastered a bashful expression on her face, one she had seen her mum use more times than she cared to remember. She detected the discreet movement of Rhys' eyes downwards where she knew the neckline of her top gaped open slightly. *Caught you.*

She smiled over at Rhys as she sat back in her chair, making sure she was still looking as she slowly crossed her denim-covered legs. Operation "get her attention" was definitely underway. *I can do this; I can do this. I can—*

Several heads turned to look when the classroom door opened, and Amy poked her head inside, smiling as always. "Hey, do you have room for one more?"

"Yes! Welcome!" Rhys made the beckoning sign with her hands for *welcome* and stood up to let Amy take her chair. Amy looked around the circle and gave Scarlet a grin.

Scarlet tried to school her features, but she felt the blood drain from her face. She subconsciously tugged on her scarf so it covered her chest, feeling exposed.

With only about ten minutes of the class left, Scarlet busied herself with practising the signs they'd been using. Rhys had shown them a BSL app they could download, which was like a database of searchable video clips, and Scarlet used it to look up some other job signs. When everyone gathered their things at the end of class, Scarlet hurried to join them. Amy's arrival had thoroughly thrown a spanner in the works of her plan to hang around to talk to Rhys. Putting her coat back on, she slid the papers into her bag. She was nearly at the door, about to slip out of the room, when Amy called out to her. "Scarlet, hi! Ree said you missed a few weeks of class, so let me give you those sheets. I'm sure you're going to catch up so quickly;You're picking it up really well."

For a second Scarlet was shocked to see how casually Amy went over to Rhys' bag and leafed through the folders inside. *That's just something people in relationships do.*

Amy turned back to her with half a dozen sheets of paper in her hand, smiling triumphantly. "Here you go; so, you've got this set here which is locations and where people live. Some places have their own signs, like London." She made the gesture most people would associate with "crazy" next to her head. "Or Scotland." The sign she made looked like someone compressing bagpipes under their arm.

"Thanks."

"Oh, and this is the set from last week, 'Family Members' and 'Numbers'." She ran through a few of the signs on the sheet, Scarlet was relieved to see she wasn't wearing a ring when she touched her ring finger for the sign for "husband/wife."

"Are there any other sheets you need? I think these are all the ones you missed. I hope you're okay now? I guess you came down with the bug that was going around. . .Ree didn't tell me what was wrong, just that you missed a few weeks. She's all about the confidentiality and doesn't talk about her students at home."

At home. As in, they live together.

"Woah, Amy, slow down." Rhys had finished talking to another student and returned to Amy's side. She smiled and squeezed her around the waist. "Take a breath, love." She turned to Scarlet. "Scarlet, I think you already know my girlfriend Amy?"

Scarlet noted with dismay that although Rhys said "girlfriend" she made the sign for "wife" by tapping her ring finger.

Well, that ends that plan then, doesn't it? There was no way she could go through with trying to seduce Rhys now. *Amy's my friend, I can't ruin the relationship of someone I care about.*

Her mother's voice, the devil on her shoulder, cursed her for not being selfish and thinking about rescuing her failing grades. But she was trying to be a better person. Being a better person did not involve breaking up a happy relationship for her own gains. Perhaps she needed to think not just about her failed module but about her long-term goals.

Chapter Twenty-Five

The website was sleek and professional, a net to draw in clients no doubt.

Marie spent the last few days researching, but she quickly snapped her laptop shut when Greg came into the kitchen. She was looking for a lawyer to help her make a case against the university, but she couldn't let Greg see that side of her personality, so instead she smiled at him as he started telling her about his day at the dental surgery. He was halfway through a story about a grandmother trying to wrestle a glossy magazine out of her grandchild's hands before they could read something salacious out loud in the waiting room when Marie had a lightbulb moment. *Instead of wading through hundreds of law firms, I should look up media reports of similar scandals and see who the articles listed as the legal representation for the victims!*

She patted Greg's hand and returned to her internet search.

A couple of days later, Marie was home alone preparing for a Skype meeting with the lawyer she identified as being the best to win her case against Dr Hunter and the university. She was hoping to get things moving as soon as possible and give her bank balance a much-needed boost. She was living in her overdraft all the time now, and even her monthly stipend from Scarlet's father wasn't making a dent in it. So far Greg had been resistant to moving in with her, so there was no splitting of the bills there yet either. Something needed to change and soon.

Her laptop chimed to tell her she had an incoming video call, and she schooled her features before clicking to accept. The screen filled with the face of the firm's top lawyer. In her fifties, Pamela Ng had stylishly dyed silver hair that hung straight down to her shoulders. Marie brushed her own hair back behind her ear, self-conscious in front of this well put together woman.

"Mrs Maxwell," the woman addressed Marie. "I'm pleased to make your acquaintance. I'm Pamela Ng, I understand you asked for me because of my work on the Thompson case? I have the notes my assistant took from you, but please do run me through the situation in your own words."

Marie took a deep breath and launched into the story she had been practicing all morning. She was going to be treading a very fine line here, and so much depended upon on this high profile lawyer taking the case.

"Oh Ms Ng, do you mind if I call you Pamela?" The silver head on the screen gave a slight shake. "Well, Pamela, my sweet daughter Scarlet started her first year at Dalesbury this September. I was so proud of her, you know? Going out into the world to make her own way and learn about independence. But right from the beginning she has been, well, I'm not sure how to say it."

"Go on, Mrs Maxwell, you say whatever you need to, in whatever words come easiest to you."

"There's this teacher—well, she's not just a teacher —she's the department head of Scarlet's course, and she —" Marie pressed her fisted hand to her mouth. "That woman has—" She sucked in a breath and then exclaimed, "Taken advantage of my little girl!"

Pamela's face remained stoic on the screen. "I'm sorry to press you, Mrs Maxwell, I know it can be difficult to say, but I need to know exactly what we're talking about here."

Marie patted her eyes with a tissue. "Pamela, she seduced my Scarlet! Made her do things a mother shouldn't know about. Oh, I don't know the dirty details, but I do know this teacher is having sex with my daughter! I suspect she's blackmailing Scarlet into sex. Why else would Scarlet do it? Perhaps she's told Scarlet she'll give her a failing grade if she doesn't comply. Oh my poor baby, being blackmailed into sex! It's disgusting to think I entrusted my precious daughter to that university, where she should have been safe. But she's been preyed on by a member of staff! Eurgh!"

"How old is Scarlet, Mrs Maxwell?"

"She's just turned nineteen. I know she's technically an adult, but you have to understand, she's my baby. I feel the university has violated our trust, just like their teacher has violated my daughter!" Marie sobbed into her tissue. She was putting on an excellent show, even if she said so herself.

"Okay, Mrs Maxwell, here's what—"

"I don't even think it was just seducing her with the promise of a good grade, I think that woman hurt my baby! I wanted to go to Dalesbury last week to take Scarlet out for lunch, and she refused to see me. She claimed to have a bug, but she wouldn't video call with me like we usually do. Perhaps she was hiding a black eye, or worse! Perhaps that woman hit my sweet girl!"

"Mrs Maxwell, I'm going to send my assistant to speak to Scarlet. We need to take a statement from her, and I think it would be best for her to speak with a girl closer to her own age. Don't tell Scarlet that she's coming; we don't want her to worry about it or start concocting a story to protect her, um," the serious woman shifted in her seat, looking for the right word. "Teacher."

"Why would she do that? I've told you, my poor daughter is the victim in this!"

"Yes, Mrs Maxwell, but sometimes victims don't quite see it that way. Have you heard of Stockholm Syndrome?"

"Yes, but my daughter hasn't been kidnapped and locked in a basement!"

"It's a little more complicated than that, Mrs Maxwell. But my assistant is very well qualified to get a statement from Scarlet, so try not to worry."

"Good, that's good. Thank you, Pamela." Marie leaned closer to her laptop screen. "So where will we go from there, once you have Scarlet's statement?"

"Where do you see this going?"

"Well, the Thompson case was very, um, high profile." Marie supplicated, "I thought with your reputation as leverage we could petition the faculty to remove that woman from her post, and perhaps a nice settlement from the university to keep the scandal away from their doors? Scarlet won't be able to continue on there. She'll have to start her course over again at a different uni. That means she'll be starting her post-graduate employment a year later than planned. A year's prospective salary is surely the absolute minimum she should be compensated for this disgusting breach of trust, plus the ongoing therapy she'll need to pay for."

Pamela looked at Marie through the screen with slightly narrowed eyes, an expression kept discreet by their natural almond shape. "I see. Well, thank you, Mrs Maxwell. I think this will work out nicely for both of us. Please can you ready the evidence of your daughter's abuse? My assistant will be in touch."

Pamela ended the video call, leaving Marie to stare at herself in the blank screen. She tossed the crumpled tissue to the table. This called for a celebration. She retrieved her wineglass from the worktop and sat back at the table in front of her laptop. As always, she had some online shopping tabs open at the top of the browser, and she clicked on each in turn, scanning through her wish lists and calculating what amount Greg wouldn't notice on his credit card.

Chapter Twenty-Six

"Scarlet, darling! How are you getting on?" Scarlet groggily peered at the clock in her bedroom, which read 23:38. She calculated she'd probably been asleep for about twenty minutes before the phone woke her.

"Mum? It's late. Are you okay?" She listened hard for the telltale signs that Marie was drinking. She could normally detect the slight slur in her mum's voice and at this time of night some ice cubes clinking in a glass.

"Oh yes, darling, I'm feeling really good today. How did your little date go? Did you have a nice time? Was she everything you'd hoped she would be?"

Scarlet rubbed her eyes, "There was no date, mum—"

"What on earth happened, Scarlet? You were all set to go out to drinks with her this evening, weren't you? You couldn't even get that right, could you?" Marie snapped through the phone, then muttered, "How can you be a daughter of mine?"

"No, mum, I'm sorry. Listen, I was all set to ask her to go for drinks with me. I dressed up like you told me and made sure to get her to notice me. But then her girl-friend turned up at the end of class, and they are serious mum. Like, *really* serious."

"Scarlet," Marie scoffed, "You have to work harder, obviously it wasn't enough to dress in whatever you deem to be *nice* clothes and bat your eyelashes a bit. You've let yourself go since the summer, a winter coat isn't an excuse to gain weight, Scarlet."

"I haven't, mum!"

"Oh, really? Your clothes were looking awfully snug when I last saw you. What have you been eating? Pizza, I bet. You know what carbs do to you, darling. You need to go low carb again and hit the gym. Don't get soft! I'm only watching out for you, Scarlet. Listen to the benefit of my experience; you only have youth on your side for a limited amount of time, and then you'll have an uphill struggle for everything you want. Trust me on this, darling."

Okay, so instead of completely drunk mum, I'm being treated to mildly drunk and ranting mum. What a pleasure.

Closing her eyes, Scarlet threw in the odd "Mmm hmm" whenever her mother stopped to take a breath. She'd nearly dozed back to sleep when she suddenly registered her mother telling her that if she hadn't managed to sleep with Rhys, then it was her own fault for not being pretty or thin enough. "If you haven't managed to get the goods, then you're going to have to make the evidence of your affair on your own."

"What?!"

"Just what I said, darling. You're going to need to get some evidence and fast. I've arranged for a lawyer to take your case."

"Mother!"

"It's too late now, darling, it's all arranged. Just do what I did when I was seeing that guy. . .what was his name?" Scarlet could hear her mother tapping her nails against the phone. "Steve! That's right, Steve. Do you remember him? Anyway, I 'borrowed' his phone and sent myself some naughty messages. He was none the wiser, but it worked out nicely when I threatened to tell his wife if he didn't pay off my credit card. That's what you need to do darling, borrow her phone out of her bag, or jacket or wherever lesbians like her keep their phones. Not the sort to carry a handbag is she?"

"How do you know that she's not the sort to carry a handbag?"

"Oh, I know the sort of woman you go after, Scarlet," Marie brushed the question aside. "You have a type. I'm not saying there's anything wrong with that, you like what you like." Marie's alcohol intake must have increased while they had been talking because a slur had crept into her voice.

"That was a very specific observation, mother. Wait, have you met her?!"

"What? Oh, maybe just briefly, darling. But don't worry; she didn't know who I was. I didn't even know it was her until you mentioned the name of that damn dog. She was trying to get me out of my car after the crash, but it was raining, darling!"

Scarlet sat up in bed. "Crash?! What crash, mum?"

"Oh Scarlet, it's not for you to worry about. Who's the parent here? Anyway, I need you to get her phone. . .send yourself some messages. They need to be good, Scarlet. Show evidence of her persuading you into sex. Perhaps telling you she can arrange for you to fail the class, or be kicked out of uni if you don't agree to sleep with her."

"Mother, that's"—*Horrendous. Evil*—"criminal".

"It probably won't ever get used in court, darling; we just need the evidence, and then the uni will agree to a settlement to keep the scandal out of the media. Besides, it would be a civil case, not a criminal one."

Scarlet was stunned. She never thought this would get so out of hand. "That's really what this is about? Getting money out of the university? The university where I'm doing my degree? This is my future we're talking about here, mum!"

"Oh, for goodness' sake, Scarlet, I'm doing this for

you. Think of the payout this is going to get us. I wouldn't do this for loose change. This will be major money. The lawyer I've found is excellent; her reputation is impeccable. Just her name is going to scare the university into settling out of court."

"Mum, seriously this is like nothing you've done before. What were you thinking? This is so much bigger than us."

"It's done now, darling. I've instructed the lawyer. Just be a good girl and give your statement to her assistant when she comes to see you. You must go through with this." She paused for effect and then added, "unless you want me to lose the house."

"The house?"

"Well, I had to use something to pay the retainer for the legal team, but as soon as we get the payout from the university the lawyer will take her fees from that and the house will be safe. You wouldn't want to be responsible for us losing the house, would you, Scarlet?"

"Of course not, mum, but this is just so far removed—"

"Good, darling; make sure you really play it up for the legal team, ok? That woman coerced you into having sex with her by threatening to kick you out of uni, didn't she, my poor darling?"

"But it's not true! I don't think I can lie like that, mum."

"It's not lying, darling; it's acting." With that Marie

hung up, leaving Scarlet with a sense of dread in the pit of her stomach.

I can't do this.

She reached for the glass of water on her bedside table and went to take a sip. Her stomach roiled, and she bolted off the bed, across the hall to the bathroom, retching over the toilet until she was sure there was nothing to come up.

Sitting on the side of the bath, she pressed a cold flannel against the back of her neck. One of her knees bounced up and down uncontrollably, and she shivered. A soft knock sounded at the bathroom door, and Lily called her name.

"I'm fine, Lil, honestly. You don't need to come in. Go back to sleep."

"Are you sure? I can get you a slice of toast or something? It might settle your stomach." *Precious Lily,* Scarlet thought, *she's going to be a brilliant midwife. She is so caring and naturally seems to know how to look after people.*

"Actually, Lil, a slice of toast does sound really good. Thank you."

"Coming right up!" Lily said, and then laughed and added, "Well, hopefully it *won't* come back up. You know what I mean, hun."

"Right, yeah." Scarlet wrung out the flannel and swilled some water around her mouth, cringing at the bitter taste. She grabbed her toothbrush and promised

Lily she would come downstairs once she had freshened up.

Cutlery clattered as Lily busied herself with making cups of tea and toast while Scarlet sat down at the kitchen table. She dropped her head into her hands and sighed.

"Is something bothering you, Scarlet? You can talk to me, you know." Empathy warmed Lily's voice.

Scarlet thought about telling her the whole sorry story, but she was too shocked and embarrassed to confide in her friend, so she smiled thinly at Lily as she put the plate of toast down in front of her. "I'm fine, just an upset stomach. It was probably the sandwich I grabbed from the reduced shelf in the shop earlier."

Lily sat next to her and rubbed Scarlet's arm. Her fingers were warm from holding her mug of tea. Their warmth smoothed the goosebumps that'd covered Scarlet's skin since speaking to her mother.

Chapter Twenty-Seven

Worry filled Scarlet for the next few days. Nerves hounded her. The thought of the interview with the legal team was never far from her mind. She wasn't sure when they would make contact. Her mother hadn't known when it would be.

Alongside the worry about the train wreck that conversation would turn out to be, she'd also been thinking about the crash comment Marie accidentally let slip out. *Mum crashed her car; that must have been why she was driving Greg's car while her Audi was in the garage.*

Then after the crash she'd met Rhys? And Peggy? How did that play into all of this?

To top it all off, another piece of coursework landed in her diary. She had a week to find an article on Westermarck's 1891 hypothesis and then write an argument for or against it as it related to modern psychological theory. How was she going to get through the next few days with everything swimming around in her head? She had no appetite and had lived off coffee for the last 48 hours. At least her mum would be happy if she lost a few pounds.

There was also the nagging dread in her stomach about the *evidence* she was supposed to get. How could she do that to Rhys and Amy?

She'd definitely begun to think of Amy as more of a friend than just an acquaintance. And what if her mother's plan came together? Would she get kicked out of uni? She'd have to tell her friends what happened. What would they think of her?

They would be disgusted with me.

Scarlet felt pretty disgusted with herself, if she was honest. She wanted so badly to stand up for herself, to stand up to her mother. Why could she never stand up to Marie? It was like Stockholm Syndrome. She had lived with Marie's idiosyncrasies for so long that they were her norm. They'd worn her down over time, and now she was just worn out.

It turned out Scarlet was at home eating a bowl of cereal for lunch, as students often do, when she received the phone call asking her to meet Pamela Ng's assistant at a suite of rented offices in Dalesbury city centre. They gave her the address and told her Hannah

Hoffman would expect her at three o'clock that afternoon.

From one until two, Scarlet oscillated between trying to decide what to wear to the meeting and trying not to be sick.

At half past two, she parked in the multi-storey car park and sat in her car for fifteen minutes shaking like a leaf.

At 2:47, she psyched herself up enough to get out of the car on trembling legs, and make her way across the street to the office building.

The male receptionist called up to the office Hannah Hoffman rented for this meeting. He was a broad man with an immaculately groomed beard. His office chair creaked under his weight as he swung around to grab something from the printer behind him.

Scarlet sat in one of the low padded chairs, waiting for the assistant to come down to fetch her. She crossed and uncrossed her legs. Her body needed some kind of outlet for the pent up nerves coursing through her. This really was the worst thing her mother had ever gotten her into. She resolved to sort out how their relationship would have to change once this nightmare was over.

"Hello, Scarlet?"

Scarlet whipped her head towards the person who had addressed her. At first she thought the woman coming down the stairs was leaving an appointment. She had expected the assistant to a legal juggernaut like Pamela Ng to be wearing a power suit. This girl looked to be only a few years older than Scarlet herself. She, Hannah, was wearing expensive black jeans and a blazer over a simple white t-shirt. When Hannah reached out to shake her hand, Scarlet's eyes flicked down to the chunky Rolex on her wrist.

Okay, so probably born into money, enough money that she didn't need to intimidate people with a business suit. It was probably her family's influence that had landed her this job, perhaps they had insisted she work a "proper job" rather than just living off the family's money. Scarlet looked into her face and wondered if she was right.

Hannah smiled at her. "It's a pleasure to meet you, Scarlet. I wish it were under better circumstances."

"It's good to meet you, too. And I wish none of this were happening."

"Okay, well, let's go upstairs, and we'll see what we can get sorted out."

For the next two hours Hannah walked Scarlet through her statement, step by agonising step. The offices were generic rent-a-desk spaces, with two more of the padded chairs on one side of the room and a more traditional desk on the other.

They sat in the chairs and Hannah took notes on an iPad while Scarlet talked. She had to pause often, not knowing what to say. *What is the right thing to say when you're being forced to lie about someone you like?*

Someone genuinely nice, who can't help the fact they've inadvertently been painted into an acquaintance's fantasy?

She didn't *want* to get Rhys into trouble, but her loyalty was to Marie. She couldn't let her mum lose their house. She'd felt responsible for them both ever since her mum's second divorce. Scarlet had been ten. It was when Marie started drinking earlier and earlier in the day. A ten-year-old taking on the burden of keeping the house clean and cooking for them both had been tough. Her mother seemed to be able to exist on a few bits of cheese and crackers as long as there was a bottle of wine to go with it. She didn't acknowledge that a growing girl needed better nutrition and more importantly, the attention of her only parent.

Hannah's notes were filled with Marie's lies. Marie had instructed Scarlet on exactly what to say; her attention finally focused on her daughter. She even told her that when she didn't know what to say crying was the perfect placeholder. It would seem that she was just too distressed by what had happened to get her words out.

I've always wanted mum's attention.. I want to feel like I'm important to her. Scarlet wished she could be important to her mother in a positive way, and not just because Marie could finally make some money out of her.

Exhaustion washed over Scarlet when they finally finished. Her head hurt, and she pressed the sleeve of her jumper under her puffy eyes. Hannah gave her a sympathetic look as she flipped the cover over her iPad. "Don't worry too much. Pamela will have the university quaking in their boots. There's no way they'll let this go to court;they'll settle to make it all go away."

"Are you sure? I feel so stupid."

"Yes, I'm sure, and no, you're not stupid. This woman, Dr Hunter, should have more self control than to go after her students like this. I know you're an adult, but she's still in a position of power at the university. It's not on."

"Thanks." Scarlet turned her face away in shame; she hoped Hannah would see it as an act of embarrassment and not see her for the liar she was.

Hannah reached out and touched Scarlet's arm. She turned and looked into the confident eyes of the older woman. "Listen, I know this is the last thing you need right now, but when this has all blown over and you're not my boss's client anymore, perhaps you'd like to go out for dinner sometime?"

Scarlet's eyes went wide, and she choked out a laugh which turned into proper choking as she breathed in her own saliva. *Attractive.*

"Me?" She squeaked, completely taken aback.

"Yes, you. I know how this could come across, you've been taken advantage of once already, and you're vulnerable right now. I promise that I'm sincere in wanting to get to know you."

Well, that was a surprise, Scarlet thought as she drove back home. Hannah had been charming, but Scarlet had been too preoccupied with all the lying, and the crying, to notice how Hannah regarded her. In hindsight, the other woman's gaze had lingered on her, but she'd chalked that up to Hannah watching for signs she was lying.

Finally she had been shown interest by someone who her mother would approve of, someone clearly wealthy, and their meeting was tangled up in the storm Marie created.

It would be best to wait before mentioning Hannah to her mother.

Chapter Twenty-Eight

Compartmentalising was a skill Scarlet was quickly having to become good at. She decided to carry on with her coursework as though nothing was going on, on the off chance that her mother didn't completely ruin her life and get her kicked out of uni. She had the critical analysis to write on Westermarck, and she knew she needed to get a decent mark on it to get her overall grade up.

Lily had an essay to write, too, so they both packed up their bags for a whole day in the campus library. Lily made sure they had flasks of coffee, sandwiches, and several snacks each. She had it all lined up on the kitchen table and was rummaging around in the back of the cupboard for bottled water when Scarlet came downstairs. "Wow, Lil. I feel like a kid being sent off on a school trip!"

"Well, we need brain food to keep us going."

"I'm not sure chocolate biscuits count as brain food."

"They so do! Chocolate has antioxidants. Anyway, I don't think we need an excuse to eat a good chocolate biscuit."

"True," Scarlet acquiesced.

Lily's chocolate biscuits did help for the first half of their essay marathon, but as the afternoon wore on Scarlet's mind drifted. She couldn't stop thinking about the impending doom of Pamela Ng engaging the university in her mother's ridiculous war. She wished the whole situation would go away. Sometimes for a split second she would forget, but then it all came crashing back into her mind again.

I wonder when Pamela and Hannah will contact the university? Would they warn her it was happening? Or would she find out from her mother after the fact? Worse still, would she find out when Rhys got suspended? Perhaps she would just not be there one day, removed from her lecturer and department head duties. Scarlet wondered whether they would investigate the accusations, or would they just get rid of Rhys as quickly as possible? Maybe Rhys herself would prefer to leave quietly rather than dealing with being investigated.

The Green outside the window was cast in long afternoon shadows. It would start to get dark soon. She pulled her jumper tighter, feeling the chill from the large glass walls. Lily looked over at her and gave her a half smile. "Why don't you stretch your legs for a few minutes? I'll watch your stuff."

"Thanks, Lil. I do think I need to move around a bit."

For the next fifteen minutes Scarlet wandered around the reference section. She pulled out a few books to take back to her desk and hugged them as she walked. Eventually, the stiffness eased from her legs. She was about to return to her essay and the flask of coffee Lily made when Amy pushed a trolley around the corner into the aisle. Peggy trotted at her side, stopping and grinning her happy doggy grin up at her mistress each time Amy paused to return a book to its place or sort out an untidy shelf.

Amy smiled pleasantly as she worked, and when she turned her head enough to see Scarlet standing halfway down the aisle, her work smile turned into a genuinely happy one. Scarlet couldn't help but return the smile. It was infectious. She wanted so badly to be able to be standoffish with Amy and to distance herself from their budding friendship so it wouldn't hurt so much when it was all ripped away from her. But Amy was Amy, she didn't know that Scarlet — well, Scarlet's mother — was plotting the downfall of Rhys and their relationship.

Not for the first time, Scarlet wished it wasn't Amy who was involved with Rhys. *Why couldn't Rhys have a horrible girlfriend who needed to be ousted? Better yet, why couldn't Rhys be single?* She sighed and vowed that later she would devise some mental self-punishment befitting of her crimes. For now, she returned Amy's smile while telling herself to make small talk and then get out of there. Seeing Amy happy and knowing that in a short amount of time the kind librarian would be devastated made Scarlet feel sick with herself.

As Amy got closer Scarlet realised she was holding herself very tensely as she pushed the trolley. It only contained books on the top shelf, as if she couldn't bend down to the lower ones. Amy shelved the book in her hand, then pressed her fingers against the back of her neck, rubbing it with a barely disguised scowl.

Whiplash?

Everything clicked into place for Scarlet—her mother's crash, Rhys and Peggy being there. *It must have been Amy that mum hit! No doubt it was mum who had crashed into Amy and not the other way around.*

Why did her mother have to be her mother? Other people's parents weren't like Marie, but it had taken Scarlet leaving her mother's house to get her to see how different Marie really was. *Perhaps Greg will be the one to settle mum down? I won't hold my breath.*

Marie didn't think about the people she affected with her schemes. She wouldn't give a second thought to the fact that her plan to extort money from the university would crush not only Rhys' teaching reputation, but her personal life as well. In turn that would devastate

Amy, perhaps break apart their relationship if Amy didn't believe the affair was a lie. Or if Amy did believe Rhys, and they stayed together, Amy might have to leave her job at the university library. They might have to move away from their family and friends to find new jobs. Rhys wouldn't be able to teach again with her ethics called into disrepute. She would have to start over in a completely different field. They could lose their house if they didn't have enough money coming in to cover the bills.

"So this is your last essay before the Christmas break? That's exciting! Are you looking forward to having a couple of weeks off?" Amy beamed at Scarlet, then her mouth turned down slightly at the corners when she saw the expression on Scarlet's face. "Oh, no; are things not good?"

"Not really, no. It's mum, she's being very difficult at the moment. I'm not looking forward to spending Christmas with her and her new boyfriend. She'll use the festivities as an excuse not to have to hide her drinking. And she's not shy about letting me know her opinions on my life."

"Will you be safe at home?" Amy pressed. "Does she get violent when she drinks? Is it an option for you to stay in your student accommodation over Christmas?"

"Physically I'm not in any danger from her. Mentally? Eh." She shrugged her shoulders in defeat.

"Anyway, she would never hit me, she wouldn't risk damaging what she sees as another asset."

"Pardon? What do you mean, Scarlet?"

"Oh, just that it's her life's ambition to marry me off to a rich woman and bleed her dry." She replied with glib sarcasm, although Amy couldn't hear it.

"What?!" Amy exclaimed loudly, then clapped her hand over her mouth, eyes wide. "I was just really loud, wasn't I?"

"Um, yeah." Scarlet gave her an apologetic smile. Amy took her arm and abandoned the trolley of books, pulling her into an empty study pod. She turned to her with an alarmed look on her face. "Sorry I can't always regulate the volume of my voice. So, she wants to get you into some sort of Sugar Baby marriage? I didn't know things like that really happened."

"I guess you could call it that." Scarlet looked down at her feet, ashamed. "Only without the other woman knowing that that was the arrangement."

"So, more like a con?"

"Ugh, well, when you say it like that . . ." Scarlet trailed off. "That's exactly what it sounds like. Please don't tell anyone this, Amy. It's what my mum has been doing to her boyfriends for years. It's just become so normal."

"Oh, Scarlet, this is bad."

"I know, trust me, I really know." Scarlet looked pleadingly at her friend. "The longer I've been here, been away from her, the more I've begun to see her for what she is. I think she's done something really bad this time. I feel like I'm drowning."

She couldn't help the sob that escaped her when Amy pulled her into a hug. Amy was sweet and kind, and Scarlet felt the self-hatred creep further over her.

"Do you want to tell me about the bad thing?"

Scarlet pulled back from the hug so that Amy could read her lips. "I can't, not yet." Amy looked at her with such tenderness and understanding that Scarlet nearly changed her mind. "But I want to, I just need to try one last time to stop her."

"Okay," Amy smiled, "I believe in you Scarlet. You know you can do anything you set your mind to, right?"

"And if I can't, there's always the police." Scarlet didn't add that getting the police involved would get her in just as much trouble as her mother, but she was resolved now. She couldn't let Marie destroy Rhys and Amy.

Amy was becoming a real friend to her.

Chapter Twenty-Nine

Something was going to have to give. Scarlet knew she would have to do something. She couldn't allow her mother to plough through the lives of these people she cared about.

Leaving Amy staring worriedly after her, Scarlet returned to Lily, who was obliviously tapping away at her own essay.

Things felt much clearer now. While her mother's behavior was normal to Scarlet, it was far removed from what other people knew to be the sane behaviour of a parent. She needed the outside view of others to see Marie's actions for what they were. *Criminal. Truly, criminal.*

She plopped down into her chair and began gathering her things into her bag. She'd already saved her essay to the Cloud, so she logged out of the university network and shrugged into her coat.

Lily looked up at her with bleary eyes. "Are you okay, Scarlet? You look a bit flustered. I'm just about done with my first draft. Shall we grab something for dinner on our way home?"

"Anyone would think you were trying to feed me up, Lil."

"You haven't been eating well lately. I've noticed, and the others have noticed, too. I would like to see you eat a hearty meal."

"I'm sorry, Lil, but I need to go home." The resignation in her voice was enough to tell Lily she didn't mean back to their house, but rather, back to her mother's house.

"Is there anything I can do?"

"Not really, no," Scarlet sighed, "Well, actually, perhaps you could phone me tomorrow and just — I don't know — talk to me? I think I might need some sane conversation after an evening with my mother."

"I can do that."

On her drive home, Scarlet heard her phone chirp with a new message. She assumed it was Lily, so when she pulled into her mother's driveway she was surprised to see a text from Hannah, asking how she was. She smiled to herself, a genuine feeling of happiness that this near stranger was thinking of her. It was strange how comfortable she'd felt in Hannah's presence. *We clicked straight away.*

She wondered what Hannah saw in her; she was so obviously nowhere near being in Hannah's league. Hannah was rich, confident, and sophisticated. Scarlet knew she should feel insignificant around a woman like that. But the truth was, Hannah had a way of making her feel she was *more*. It was clearly a gift that she possessed, an ability to make people feel at ease. It was why she was so good at her job and able to extract difficult information from a client or witness.

When they met Scarlet assumed the warmth she felt from the other woman was down to a well-honed professional skill. But at the end of the meeting, when Hannah had smoothly asked her out, she felt a flicker of her own self esteem — normally dormant — brought to life by a couple of hours with this woman.

Marie's car was in the driveway, and Scarlet was happy to see Greg's car was absent. The lights were on downstairs, so she knew her mother hadn't gone out with Greg.

Pulling her overnight bag across from the passenger seat, she trudged towards the front door. She was dreading this confrontation with her mother. She hadn't let Marie know she was coming, and she mentally crossed her fingers that the surprise of her visit would help her cause. There was no way she could be part of this horrible plan. She couldn't sit by and let Marie do this. Complacency would feel just as bad as complicity, in the end. As she got to the door, she took a fortifying breath before putting her key in the lock and letting herself in.

Marie was in the living room, curled up on the sofa with a wine glass and a bottle of Merlot on the coffee table. A reality tv-show played slightly too loud on the TV. Marie obviously hadn't heard the front door because she jumped when her daughter addressed her. "Oh, darling, I didn't know you were here."

Thank God. I've arrived early enough at least mum's not slurring yet.

"Hi, mum. How are you?" Scarlet eased herself into the conversation she knew needed to happen. It was for the best, Marie was likely to explode at her.

"I'm okay, darling. Have you been watching this show? It's shocking!"

"No, but I've heard good things about it." Scarlet pulled off her coat and draped it over the back of the armchair. She settled in for the rest of the episode, deciding to talk to her mum when it ended. This was cosy and comfortable — time spent with her mum when Marie wasn't talking *at* her, demanding things from her, belittling her. This was what she thought a mother/daughter relationship should be like. *Every so often we have the tiniest snippet of normality in the turbulent sea that the boat of our relationship bobs about on. I'm sure these few minutes are the calm before the storm. That's an apt analogy. Perhaps I should be doing English Lit instead of Psychology?*

Scarlet was shocked when Marie didn't shout. She was quiet and listened while Scarlet told her she didn't want to be involved with Marie's plan. She didn't want to deceive the university, and she certainly didn't want to drag Rhys through the mud all for the sake of money.

This was the sort of thing Marie did, Scarlet realised. These were the behaviours Marie used to lull her daughter into a false sense of security.

"I thought I was helping you, dear. After all, how dare that woman turn you down? Does she think she's too good for you? That she's better than us?"

And now came the gaslighting. Marie would try to turn things around so it seemed like things weren't her fault, perhaps even seem like they weren't her idea at all. Scarlet was sure she hadn't done anything to encourage her mother to take such extreme actions.

Or had she?

No! That's ridiculous. That is exactly what mum wants me to think.

She needed to get away from that mindset. Now was the time to be self-aware. That's what she needed, to recognise what Marie was doing and resist falling under the spell that had been cultivated since her childhood.

Anyway, it would be fine to *think* about a tiny bit of revenge, of getting your own back on someone who'd done something bad to you. But to actually act on it in the way that Marie did was insane.

Scarlet could see that now. The distance of moving out of the house allowed her to see Marie for what she was.

She wondered what had made her mother become this person.

Unfortunately for Scarlet, a quiet Marie was far more dangerous than a loud and ranting Marie. A very quiet Marie crept into Scarlet's room after her daughter had fallen asleep. Scarlet slept deeply; it was the best night's sleep she'd had in weeks. A weight had been lifted after telling her mother she wouldn't be part of her plan.

Marie quietly unplugged Scarlet's phone from her bedside table and took it into the privacy of her own bedroom. Luckily Scarlet had never updated her passcode, so her mother still knew it from when she had diligently checked her teenager daughter's phone messages from bullies and other unsavoury characters.

Scanning through Scarlet's photos, she looked for

the selfie Scarlet had taken of Rhys' coffee cup, planning to send it to herself. She was also thrilled to find the photos Scarlet had secretly taken in Rhys' office. Her daughter was clearly recognisable, wrapped in the arms of a woman with distinctive tattoos visible below the rolled up cuff of her shirt.

Oh, you little beauty.

Marie was delighted. She had fully expected to have nothing but the coffee cup to lean on, but this was better than she could've imagined. Perhaps not quite the evidence of a sordid sexual relationship that would've condemned Rhys, and had the university running scared from Pamela's immense legal wrath, but she never would've expected her daughter to have the wherewithal to get this.

She clutched the phone to her chest briefly in relief, then sent a copy of the photos to herself. Her pounding heart quieted as she relaxed. Marie applauded herself for her restraint in dealing with Scarlet this evening. Her stress levels had risen as her daughter derailed her plan, but she was back on track now. This was something solid she could use.

Just to be on the safe side, she continued with her original plan to forge some messages on Scarlet's phone. She thanked her lucky stars she had stumbled over that *Catfish* programme. It explained how these people could harvest photos from a real person to create a fake profile, then they used the fake profile to send messages. *It was inspired!*

She'd prepared for this opportunity and already found a photo of Rhys from the university website to use as a profile picture. She'd set up the fake account a couple of days ago. Her intention had been to coordinate with Scarlet to send the bogus messages. But without Scarlet's cooperation, all she really needed was Scarlet's phone.

She constructed the message thread, sending a message as Rhys from her laptop, then replying using Scarlet's phone until she had a full, and incriminating, conversation between them.

Marie carefully took a screenshot of the conversation on Scarlet's phone and sent it to herself. Then she deleted the messages.

All she had to do now was return the phone to Scarlet's bedside table, send the evidence to Pamela's legal team, and then she could sit back and wait for the lawyer to do what she did best.

Chapter Thirty

The next morning Scarlet heard her mother leave the house, presumably to go to the Pilates class she attended every week. She rolled out of bed feeling well rested and with less anxiety than she'd felt for quite some time. After a hot shower and a quick rummage around in her bag for a clean t-shirt, she pulled on the jeans she'd taken off before bed and went downstairs to make herself some breakfast.

Her phone rang just as she was eating her toast. A glance told her it was Lily, calling like she'd promised. She grabbed the last slice off the plate and took her phone into the living room.

They talked for a few minutes about their essays, while Scarlet chewed her toast.

"Did you get some downtime after speaking to your mum?"

"Yeah, Lil. It was fine." Scarlet skirted around the problems with her home life as usual. It was too embarrassing to explain it to her friends. Deep down, she still thought they wouldn't want to be her friends anymore if they found out about her awful mother. Scarlet had a hard time not seeing herself and her mother as one entity, so she wouldn't blame anyone else for coming to the same conclusion — that Scarlet must be guilty too.

As soon as possible she steered Lily towards less loaded topics.

"So, Lil, how was your date last night?"

"It was great. He's studying radiology, so we have medical school stuff in common. I think we got on really well; I think he thought so too. And he has the nicest butt!"

"And?"

"And what do you want to know? He didn't ask me to give him a blow-job in the back of the car like the last guy I went out with. So, winning!"

"Yeah, that's an improvement."

Talking about Lily's love life reminded Scarlet about Hannah. It was unusual for her to talk about a woman with her friend. So far, during the course of their friendship, she'd only had eyes for Rhys. Of course, she couldn't talk about her. Even though Hannah was entangled with the Rhys/Marie/University extortion drama, Scarlet felt she could mention her existence as long as she didn't say how they met.

"It's very new, and might be nothing. But then again, it might turn into something. I have to have hope."

She wandered around the living room as she spoke and settled herself on the windowsill. Vaguely, she was aware her mother had returned from her morning workout. She cradled the phone against her ear and stroked the pad of her thumb over the perished rubber around the window frame. She remembered sitting here so many times as a child, how many times had she watched her mother's boyfriends leave? She didn't want that for herself, jumping from one relationship to the next, unable to stand on her own. Even though she was young, she knew her personality wasn't suited to that. She wanted a long-term relationship with the best person she could find for herself. As she told Lily this she wondered, "Perhaps that person will be Hannah Hoffman."

"Did you just say Hannah Hoffman?" Marie burst through the door of the living room, her gym bag dropping to the floor. "Scarlet, I absolutely forbid you to have anything to do with her." Scarlet was shocked at the stone cold sober look in her mother's eyes, the chill in her voice.

"I've got to go, Lil." She hung up the phone without waiting for Lily's reply.

"Mum? I thought you'd be pleased. She seems just the sort of woman you've been on at me to meet."

"How did you meet her?" Marie demanded.

"She's Pamela's assistant, she's the one who came to take my statement. What's this all about, mum?"

Marie spluttered in a most un-Marie like way.

"Her family are the most vile, self serving, egotistical philanderers I've ever had the misfortune to meet." Her face twisted in a horrible sneer, and she spat out bitterly, "They are not the sort of people you should have anything to do with. No good will ever come from those people. You have to promise me, Scarlet, you will stay far away from that Hoffman brat."

"She was really nice, mum. Even though it was a tough situation, she made me feel really relaxed. She was charming, and she asked me to go out with her once all this business is over."

Marie's face froze into a slack expression as she stared at her daughter. It took a moment for her to get her mouth working again. "But nothing's happened between you? Scarlet, please tell me nothing has actually happened!" Marie wore such a panicked look, her face turning red and blotchy, that Scarlet began to worry for her mother's health.

"Mum? I think you need to sit down and have a glass of water. You're scaring me." She pulled on her arm and tried to steer her onto the sofa.

Marie caught Scarlet's sleeve and pulled her down too. "Scarlet, listen, this is really important."

"I don't understand what the matter is, mum? This is what you've always wanted for me."

"Not with your sister!"

Scarlet sat back, stunned.

My what?

She must have misheard, misunderstood.

"I don't have a sister," she said dumbly.

Marie was visibly sweating, a cold sweat had broken out on her now pale face.

"Hannah Hoffman. Daughter of Christopher Hoffman, your father."

Scarlet blinked at her mother. She'd never heard her mother mention her father before. It was just one of those things they never spoke of. Evidently her mother knew enough about him and his life to be able to tell her this now.

A sister? A Half-sister? Hannah.

Fuck.

Chapter Thirty-One

"Scarlet, I need to explain all this to you, everything that happened with your father. What is still happening, to some extent, anyway." Marie took her daughter's hand a bit too tightly to be comfortable.

"I really think you do, mum!" Even though Scarlet was shocked by the sudden turn her day had taken, she'd always wondered about her father and the way her mother refused to talk about him. The bomb Marie had dropped about her familial relationship with Hannah was a speck of dust compared to the mushroom cloud of finding out her mother had been holding onto information about Scarlet's father all this time.

She settled in for her mother's story.

"You won't know this about me, but I once had the beginnings of a successful career in The City. I moved into central London and I worked as a personal assistant. I was so good at it, Scarlet. I moved to different companies, more prestigious than the last, until I landed a position at Hoffman and Sons. Their reputation was outstanding and my position was with the CEO's eldest son, the one who would take over the company one day. Everything was going so well for me, darling.

"But then that swine did the unthinkable! He made me fall in love with him. It would've all been so perfect if it hadn't been for his wife. She didn't treat him the way he deserved. She was pregnant, and all she thought about was herself and the baby. Something about high blood pressure and prescribed bed rest. Anyway, she wasn't servicing his needs as a man. Luckily, I was there to take her place."

"The baby was Hannah?"

"No, Hannah is their middle child, the baby was their youngest son David."

So I have more than one half sibling I knew nothing about?

"Anyway, Christopher told me many times he wished I was his wife instead of that bitch. I asked him to divorce her and marry me. He was rich enough to pay her off and not even notice the difference in his bank balance. The problem was his father. Mr Hoffman senior is an old-fashioned family man through and through. There was no way he would allow his son to divorce his pregnant wife. When Christopher suggested separating from her, his father threatened to cut him off. He would've been forced out of the company, and his younger brother would have inherited everything instead. His father had him over a barrel; he knew how important the inheritance was to Christopher. He staked the company's wholesome reputation on his own son's greed. Even when I found out I was pregnant with you, darling, your father wouldn't go against Mr Hoffman. He wouldn't risk being disinherited. He didn't love us enough. He loved his money more.

"Yes, of course, I was heartbroken at first, but then I woke up one day and decided to use his greed myself. I was going to start showing soon, and I told him I would leave him and the company quietly if he provided for us with a monthly payment. No one at work would know I was pregnant, and so there would be no speculation about his reputation."

"You blackmailed my father?"

"Blackmail is such a harsh word. No, it was more like a child maintenance payment, darling. Remember, he knew all about you and he wanted to shut me up and get rid of us both. I didn't keep you from him. He wanted the whole situation to disappear, and he used money to do that. He is not a good man, Scarlet. As soon as we threatened his comfortable existence, he turned on us.

"So now you know the whole sorry situation; I was so close to getting that perfect lifestyle, but his wife and children were a barrier I couldn't overcome. I'm sorry about that, darling. I tried my best."

Marie gave a deep sigh of relief, like she had shrugged off the weight of the world from her shoulders. Slapping her hands onto her thighs, she stood with a laugh. "Oh, I feel much better for having told you that, darling. It's been eating away at me all these years. I'm glad we had this chat!"

Scarlet stared at her mother's retreating form, stunned into silence at what she'd learned. She wanted to move, to storm after her mother, but she was frozen to her seat. A few minutes later Marie popped her head back into the living room, ice cubes clinking in the glass in her hand. "Oh, and darling? Don't tell Hannah about us. I can't have Christopher stopping that payment. I can get that out of him until his father dies and he inherits. He can't have the old man changing his will, can he? Ha!"

"I'm sorry, mum, this is a massive shock. I think I need to be on my own to process all of this." She got up stiffly. Feeling like she'd been sitting there for days, Scarlet had to work hard to get her legs to cooperate as she slowly made her way up the stairs to her room and closed the door. Only then did she lean her head against the cool wood and cried.

This was too much to comprehend all on her own. Having a sister to share all this rubbish with actually sounded pretty good to her right now. In fact, she had three half siblings according to Marie. A whole family who didn't know she existed. She wanted to wonder what they were like, but Marie's warning to keep away from them rang in her ears.

How am I going to explain to Lily? She'd just been talking about the excitement of meeting someone new, someone who'd asked her out. She couldn't tell Lily the truth. It sounded ridiculous even to Scarlet — her new love interest was actually her secret half-sister, but *shhh don't tell her* that!

So, along with everything else, she was going to have to give Hannah the cold shoulder and hope she managed to just drop off her radar. It wouldn't be that simple, Hannah was intrinsically linked to them for the immediate future as Pamela's assistant.

Scarlet hoped they could lay this business to rest as quickly as possible. She was not a good actress. She just wanted to be a normal person with a normal life.

Why was *this* her life?

Chapter Thirty-Two

Sitting at the desk in her office, Rhys flicked back and forth between two tabs on her browser. One was research for her latest book; the other was a holiday cottage website showing listings near Amy's parents in Suffolk. She tapped the mouse as she pondered the dates. *Should we drive there on Boxing Day, or wait until the day after?*

She wanted the trip to be a surprise for Amy. Her mum and dad had moved to the East Coast a couple of years ago, and they hadn't been able to visit them over Christmas yet. Last year Peggy had a litter of puppies over the Christmas holidays. They were all being trained to become hearing dogs, too. Thinking about them made Rhys feel proud; Peggy was an amazing asset to Amy. They were lucky to have her as part of their family.

She clicked back onto the page she'd been using to look up some organisations she needed to contact for her research. She was just reaching for the phone on her desk to call the first number when it made her jump by actually ringing. The desk phone never rang. It was a relic she used when she was doing research and needed to call overseas numbers that weren't included on her mobile phone plan.

Frowning at the noisy object, she picked up the receiver. "Hello? Rhys Hunter speaking."

"Yes," the clipped voice of the Dean's secretary came through the phone. "Dr Khatri would like to see you in his office, Dr Hunter."

"Okay, Linda." Rhys started opening up the calendar app on her phone, "Does he have a day and time in mind?"

"You misunderstand, Dr Hunter, he wants to see you now." Linda hung up, leaving Rhys to put the phone slowly back down in its cradle. She looked at it out the corner of her eye, like it might suddenly ring again.

What was that all about? She wasn't aware of any pending matters she needed to see the Dean about.

Rhys wasn't prone to spells of anxiety, but being called before Dr Khatri at short notice was a bit worrying. *I haven't forgotten to submit the department's module outlines for next semester, have I?*

She stood and shrugged on her jacket. The administration building was across The Green and the late November day was cool. She felt an inexplicable chill she couldn't quite explain. Perhaps it was a sense of foreboding? A queasy feeling settled in her gut. *You don't just get called into the Dean's office at the drop of a hat. Something must've happened.* Maybe the plagiarism software had flagged one of her students? No matter the fact they were all aware of it — that they specifically had to upload and submit their work into the university's plagiarism programme — there was always the occasional student who believed they'd found an essay or article obscure enough to trick the system.

Perhaps he wants to talk about the funding for a research project within the department.

Wondering about it wasn't doing her any good. All she could do was get there as soon as possible and find out.

Her stomach lurched, and she wished she could've claimed not to have been on campus. That was probably why Linda had called her desk phone and not her mobile. The Dean knew that she was only a few hundred yards away, she couldn't buy time by pretending not to be there.

Unfortunately, the meeting was far worse than any of the scenarios Rhys had imagined. All the possible problems she'd thought of on the walk over from her building hadn't pertained to her personally; she'd assumed it would be about her department or her students. She could never have imagined the personal attack awaiting her in Dr Khatri's office.

Pamela had been busy since Marie sent her the screenshots from Scarlet's phone. She'd had Hannah draft a grievance letter to the University, which they submitted first thing that morning. Then, they sat back and waited for the administrative cogs of the old institution to turn.

Unethical. Predatory.

Rhys felt sick. She was none of those things. *I can't believe one of my students would accuse me of such an appalling breach of trust.*

The Dean couldn't release the name of the student who'd filed the grievance against her. Rhys wondered at that, but Dr Khatri advised her to contact her union rep before any further information was handed out. She was suspended from teaching and could only complete her admin duties from home until the outcome of the investigation.

Anger simmered. She wanted to know who'd made this accusation. This wasn't just a joke or a prank; this kind of allegation destroyed lives.

True, her students were legally adults. But she was still in a position of power over them. The statement that had been read to her claimed she had threatened to have the student removed from the university if they refused to have a sexual relationship with her.

Abhorrent.

Vile.

It was repulsive to her that anyone would think she was capable of that kind of evil manipulation.

What will Amy think? Amy will believe me, won't she?

This was about to turn Amy's world upside down too.

Amy had done an early shift, so Rhys had the whole drive home to work through what she would tell her girlfriend. She gripped the steering wheel tightly and gritted her teeth.

The Dean thinks I've been shagging one of my students.

A student has accused me of blackmailing them into sex.

I'll never be able to teach again because a student is spreading disgusting lies about me. We're going to have to move away, where no one recognises me.

How was I supposed to protect myself from something like this?

Rhys let herself in through her front door, putting down her laptop bag and keys in the hallway. Her eyes burnt with unshed tears. She took a few steadying breaths before she called out Amy's name, knowing Peggy would alert her girlfriend to her presence.

She found Amy in the kitchen cooking dinner; it smelt amazing, and she felt a stab of disappointment and guilt that they wouldn't be sitting down to enjoy it as Amy had planned.

"Baby, I'm sorry. Can you turn the stove off, please? There's something I need to talk to you about."

Amy turned towards the door to greet her, but the smile on her face dissolved as she read her girlfriend's lips. She took in Rhys' tense face and the haunted look in her eyes, and she noticed she was barely holding back tears.

"Will you come sit on the sofa with me? I need you to hold me." Rhys reached out to her, and Amy noticed her hands were shaking, explaining why she was speaking instead of signing.

"Ree? You're scaring me. What's the matter?" Rhys managed a sign then, just one.

Bad.

The tears came. They came from Rhys, and they came from Amy.

They sat curled together on the sofa with Peggy pressed against Amy's side. Peggy whined softly in her own doggy incantation of a human cry. Her humans were hurting, and all she could do to help was offer the comfort of her presence.

Rhys had talked, signing as she spoke. Amy watched

her hands and lips. But she also watched her girlfriend's body language. She knew how vulnerable Rhys felt by the press of her body against Amy's own. She wanted to wrap Rhys up in her arms. That would come later when Rhys finished talking. For now, she needed a small amount of space to see what Rhys was saying. It hurt her to see Rhys hurting, and for the first time in a long while, she cursed her inability to hear. She could see how Rhys' body desperately sought the comfort of hers.

Once Rhys finished explaining what she'd been told at the meeting, Amy asked her own questions.

"Do you have any idea which student might've made the allegation?"

No.

"Have you contacted your union rep?"

Yes.

Do you need me to collect anything from your office?"

No.

Once she'd asked all of her practical — typical Amy — questions, she guided Rhys into their bedroom. She tucked her into bed with Peggy at her feet and slipped back into the kitchen. Amy packed the forgotten dinner away into the fridge, knowing neither of them had much of an appetite anymore. Before closing the fridge door, she grabbed them each a carton of protein shake and took them into the bedroom.

Amy climbed under the covers, nudging Peggy with

her foot. Rhys turned towards her, and took the drink Amy offered, with a confused look on her face. Amy said, "We've both missed dinner. I don't think either of us can manage food right now, but we need to have some kind of sustenance. You'll need to keep your strength up to fight this shit; you can't have emotional strength if your body isn't strong."

Amy watched Rhys finish her drink while she sipped her own. Rhys usually drank these before her morning run, but Amy wasn't a fan of the thick texture. She made sure Rhys finished all of it before she curled up against Amy's side, letting her girlfriend stroke her hair as she fell into a fitful sleep.

Chapter Thirty-Three

What little sleep Rhys got that night she knew she owed to the comforting presence of her girlfriend. Amy was there, a beautiful constant in the storm, coaxing her back to sleep each time she woke. She kissed her head, stroked her arm, and entwined their feet beneath Peggy's warm little body at the bottom of the bed.

Normally her alarm would have been set for 6:30. Enough time for a quick 5 km run, then a shower and breakfast before heading into work. There would be none of that this morning, Amy had turned off her alarm. Rhys had a meeting with several of the university administrators, but not until eleven o'clock.

Amy slipped out of bed quietly, went into the kitchen to let Peggy outside, and made coffee. While the coffee dripped she video called her boss and told her she needed to take a personal day for a family emergency.

She put Peggy's food down and sat at the kitchen table for a few minutes with a steaming mug in her hands. She usually loved this time of the morning, peaceful before a busy day at work. Today was going to be a very different kind of day, and the stress of it was already starting to seep in. She watched the swirls of steam rise from her drink, made extra strong this morning in deference to her broken night of sleep.

Lost in her own thoughts, she didn't see Rhys come into the room in her running gear. She wasn't aware of her presence until Rhys slipped into the chair next to her and touched her hand. Amy gave her girlfriend a wan smile, her eyes sad. "You're going for a run?"

"Yes, I need to. I can't just lie in bed waiting to go to this meeting. I need to do something normal."

"Okay, love, but be careful? Don't do a new route."

"No, it'll just be a quick one. Out to the pavilion and back, I promise." She reached over and kissed Amy, adjusted the strap of her smartwatch on her wrist, and went into the hallway to put on her trainers. Amy leaned to the side in her chair so she could watch her as she laced her shoes. Then with a quick wave, Rhys slipped out the front door.

Peggy finished her breakfast and came to sit at Amy's side. She knew her owner was sad, and she rested her head on her lap, showing solidarity with her human.

It was cold when Scarlet woke up that morning. When she pulled open the curtains, there was frost on the windows, which made her want to go back to bed. She'd returned to her student house last night. She couldn't be under the same roof as her mother right now. She needed to process what she'd learned about her father and about Hannah.

She snorted. *Of course, something mum did twenty years ago is coming back to haunt us both.* The irony was if Marie had never come up with this crazy plan to extort money from the university, she never would've hired Pamela and Hannah. In turn, Scarlet never would have met her half-sister, never would've been asked out by her, and never would've had to turn down a woman who wore a watch that cost more than Scarlet's car. *No, that's mum's way of thinking.* It still pained Scarlet to have to lie to Hannah about why she definitely wouldn't be going out with her.

She wondered about the family that she'd never known existed until yesterday. *I actually have a dad, and at least three half-siblings.* Marie had been keen to point out there could be other illegitimate children of Christopher Hoffman, just like Scarlet. *I might never know how big my family really is. Of course, I'll never know. I can never ask my father.* Marie had been very clear on that point, too; she was never to attempt to contact the Hoffmans about any of this. Be polite to Hannah when they had dealings with her, but no communication that wasn't related to their case. Marie's advice was it was best to just fade away, be remembered as just another client, if they were even remembered at all.

Scarlet decided she needed a big bowl of sugary cereal to start her day. Her mother could make digs about weight gain to her heart's content; Scarlet needed it to perk her up for this grey day. She headed downstairs after getting dressed in a chunky-knit jumper and jeans.

Kemi was the only one at the table when she came into the kitchen. Scarlet eyed her steaming mug of coffee in envy and quickly set about making one for herself. The sugary breakfast could wait a few more minutes.

She leaned against the counter and took a sip from her mug, even though the liquid was still far too hot to drink comfortably. Still, she closed her eyes and hummed to herself at that first bit of caffeine.

"You look like you needed that," Kemi said, observing her from the other side of the room.

"Yeah, can't start the day without it." Scarlet cradled the mug in both hands, deciding not to tellKemi she hadn't been sleeping well lately. *I don't need to open that can of worms.*

She heaped her bowl with honey nut cornflakes and sat at the table to dig in. She was halfway through the cereal when her phone dinged with a text. She paused to pull it out of her pocket, frowning as she read the message.

"Is something wrong?" Kemi asked.

"Just a message from uni to say my ten o'clock lecture is cancelled. Rhys—I mean Dr Hunter—won't be in. It must be too short notice to find someone to replace her. Strange."

Scarlet pushed the phone to the side and carried on eating her breakfast.

Chapter Thirty-Four

At quarter to eleven, Rhys pulled up to the barrier of the staff car park on campus. She fumbled in the cup holder for the tag that would open the yellow and black metal arm. Her hands felt unusually cold and tingly, a physical manifestation of her anxiety. She struggled, dropping it back into the holder twice before Amy covered her fingers with her own and squeezed her hand around the small bit of plastic. Once she had the tag in her palm, all she had to do was wave it at the reader mounted outside her window and like magic the chip granted them access..

The arm raised, and they continued on towards her fate. This would be the first official meeting of several the university would have to hold.

Once they parked, Amy rested her head on Rhys'

shoulder. "We've got a few minutes. Do you want to talk through what's going to happen today?"

Rhys nodded. "In today's meeting they'll present me with the statement of grievance from the student and ask how I wish to respond to it. It will be us and Paul, Dr Khatri, and some of the uni's legal team."

Rhys had spoken to Paul, her union rep, briefly that morning and arranged to meet him in the admin building. She was entitled to have him at all the meetings. They didn't have any information yet, so he'd decided they didn't need a lengthy meeting beforehand. They would talk in more depth afterwards when they had the facts.

Amy took Rhys' hand in hers as they walked across the chilly campus. She was wearing woolly gloves and Rhys concentrated on the rough feel of the wool against her skin,grounding her. They didn't talk, both mentally preparing themselves for what the day would bring. Amy rhythmically squeezed her girlfriend's hand, and Rhys concentrated on her breathing. *Breathe in for a count of four, hold it for four, and then breathe out for four.*

Standing at the door of the building, they both took a deep breath before stepping across the threshold together, a blast of hot air hitting them as they entered. The sudden change from the outside temperature made Amy's cheeks turn pink. Normally Rhys would've told her how adorable she looked, but today she was too preoccupied.

Paul stood up from the bench in the middle of the lobby when he saw them coming and shook each of their hands. He knew Amy from the library, and the two of them exchanged small talk for a couple of minutes. Rhys tuned out their conversation, psyching herself up for what was about to happen.

"Dr Hunter? Please come in."

The conference room they entered wasn't as clinical as Amy had expected. In her mind, it was going to be a cold room with no windows and a long table. Instead, the room was light and airy with floor-to-ceiling windows looking out over the hill and down towards the train station. The lights weren't as harsh as she'd expected, either. They lit the space in a bright yet warm glow instead of the usual white glare, and the room was decorated with plants in large pots, their dark green leaves reflecting the light.

The table wasn't the traditional long one; Instead it was large and round. This was a much better set up for Amy to be able to read the lips of the other people once they were seated. When Rhys had spoken to Paul on the phone, she mentioned Amy would attend the meeting with her, and he must have arranged for the administrators to use the room that would best accommodate her communication needs. When they took their seats Amy met Paul's eye and nodded her thanks to him, then she took Rhys' hand below the table in silent support as the meeting began.

———

When the meeting was over, Rhys and Amy sat in the car before driving home. Rhys laughed ironically and said, "Part of me hoped it was a male student. At least I would've been able to point to myself and say 'but I'm really, really gay'. Then we could've all laughed about how on Earth I was supposed to prove what a massive lesbian I am."

"I know, sweetheart," Amy gave her a sad smile. "I'm sorry this is happening."

"I'm sorry, too. Perhaps I wasn't authoritative enough? Or I was too friendly, too approachable?-"

"No. Don't do that. You've done nothing wrong, Ree. Don't make excuses for her. Most people should be able to recognise niceness for what it is, not misinterpret it as flirtation. You're charming and friendly, but I don't think anyone would describe you as a flirt. Especially not with your students."

"I just can't believe it's Scarlet." Rhys said. It had shocked them both to learn who had made the allegation.

The grievance had been submitted by a lawyer who

had been instructed by Scarlet's mother. But it was fundamentally the same thing. A legal assistant from the firm, a Miss Hoffman, had attended the meeting. In a pantomime clearly meant to intimidate, she had spoken only to Dr Khatri in his role as Chair of the meeting. She made it clear that her boss, who it turned out was the infamous Pamela Ng, saw the university as a lax parent who was to blame for not keeping its delinquent child in line. Rhys was the child in this scenario, a misbehaving child who now needed to be punished for her actions. *Alleged actions.*

From what Rhys had garnered, the angle they were taking was the university as the figurehead of their grievance. They claimed a student had been coerced by a faculty member and that Dalesbury didn't have the right safeguarding framework in place to stop inappropriate relationships between their staff and students.

"I can't believe we've got to wait a week until the next meeting," Amy said.

"They've got to follow their official disciplinary procedure. In the meantime, they're using 'non-academic misconduct' to suspend me from teaching duties. For fuck's sake, I've got a department to run!"

Rhys had no doubt this was going to be a tough battle. She didn't want to voice all of her concerns to Amy. *The university will be obligated to protect their reputation, and, of course, avoid a lengthy and expensive legal battle. They might be willing to throw me under the bus to save themselves—my department's reputation and my own popularity be damned.*

"I was really starting to see Scarlet as a friend," Amy said sadly. "We've had some good conversations in the library. I felt like she was opening up to me. She seems to have some problems back at home with her mum, though. She told me she doesn't feel like her mum cares that she's moved away. I got the impression she's desperate for her mum's approval, but her mum's expectations of her are very extreme. It sounded tough."

"Her grades have been slipping, and she failed a couple of assignments this term. I had to call her into the office to tell her, but I thought she was working through it."

"Oh, I wish I'd known. Perhaps I could've spoken to her."

"That's exactly why I couldn't tell you; it would've been a breach of confidentiality. I knew you'd started to become friends, so I didn't want to put you in that position."

"This doesn't make any sense to me, Ree. I spoke to her in the library a couple of days ago. She was a little bit distant, but nothing that would've made me think she was about to accuse you of something like this. She was perfectly nice to my face. I feel a bit sick to think that under the surface she had this up her sleeve. How could she pretend to be my friend like that, and then the next minute try to destroy my partner's career? This is about you, not me, but I still feel hurt." Amy gripped onto Rhys' sleeve, desperation in her voice. They were both hurting after discovering Scarlet's duplicity.

Chapter Thirty-Five

At midday Marie texted Scarlet, asking if she would be coming home over the weekend, and if she was, would she like to have a girls' night in with a takeaway on Saturday? Scarlet always felt a bit creeped out when her mum acted nice like this. Despite always seeking her mother's approval, she got an uncomfortable feeling when it actually happened. Unfortunately, she was stuck in the cycle of always looking for the ulterior motive.

Later on there was a short message from Hannah. *Hope you're ok?*

By six o'clock Lily and Jessica came home, talking excitedly. Scarlet could hear snatched words of their conversation as she walked down the stairs, and she frowned at what they were saying.

"I heard from Charlie in the Student Union that a

member of staff's been fired for assaulting a student," Lily said.

"No, no, that's not right. I was in line in the cafe behind Gill, who works in the admin building. She was telling her friend a tutor's been suspended for having an affair with one of their students. I bet it was Gavin McCann. You know, the politics lecturer? He creeps me out. Can you imagine?" Jessica shuddered.

Scarlet stopped dead at the bottom of the stairs, her ears ringing and her vision tunnelled. She gripped the bannister tight. For a few seconds, she thought she might pass out.

Rhys being absent, her mother being nice to her, and then Hannah's message. Put together, it all made a twisted sort of sense. Marie must've pushed the "go" button.

Why did mum have to do this? Why couldn't she just stay out of my life?

Scarlet thought she was doing such a good job by moving away from Marie and making new friends, people her mother hadn't tainted. But no; Marie had found a way to wheedle into her daughter's life. And this time she managed to dig around and upset everything in an even bigger way than she ever had before.

She'd assumed the message from Hannah was a response to her own brush off a few days ago, but now it all made sense. Hannah was checking in on her because she'd served the university with the grievance.

Scarlet's first instinct was to call her mum and shout down the phone at her. This was bad, really, really bad.

Marie had taken an idea and run with it. Now Scarlet's friends would be the ones to suffer. In fact, they must already be suffering.

Scarlet couldn't bear the thought of what Rhys and Amy must be going through. This kind of allegation would destroy Rhys. It could tear their relationship apart. This wasn't just going to affect Rhys. It would affect Amy who was completely innocent in all this.

Rhys is innocent, too. Whatever my feelings towards her, I need to remember that the closeness I thought was developing between us was all in my mind. That isn't Rhys' fault.

And Amy. Sweet, compassionate Amy. Scarlet saw her as a friend. She felt like Amy was someone she could confide in. She was the only person she'd ever spoken to about her mother. Granted, Amy didn't know the half of it, but she knew a lot more than anyone else.

Do Rhys and Amy know this is my fault yet?

She had a sudden, horrible feeling that by now they probably knew. Feeling like she was going to be sick, she turned on her heel at the bottom of the stairs and fled back up. On the middle floor landing she had to swerve into Jessica and Kemi's bathroom, not able to make it up the second flight before her stomach rebelled.

She'd put out bad vibes into the universe, and now karma hit her as a physical force. She was dimly aware of her housemates calling up the stairs, "Scarlet, are you okay?" Footsteps trotted up when they heard her being sick.

Before long Lily was there, kneeling on the tiles beside her. She reached for a flannel and wet it, pressing it against Scarlet's head. "Oh, hun, I've got you. What happened?"

"Is she alright?" Jessica asked from the doorway, a sympathetic look on her face, "Seriously, babe, do you need me to run out and get you a pregnancy test?"

Choking out a laugh, Scarlet wiped her mouth with the flannel. "Um, I'm gay, remember? I'm going to buy you a new flannel, by the way."

The look of concern didn't leave Jessica's eyes, "Don't worry about it, babe, we just care about you." Then she grinned, "The offer always stands about the pregnancy test. Or condoms! Uni's a time for experimentation; yours just might be opposite to most."

"Come on, Jess." Kemi pulled her away from the door. "Leave poor Scarlet alone. She's not feeling well. She doesn't need you diagnosing her as a homoromantic pansexual right now."

Scarlet reached out and flushed the toilet, letting Lily steady her as she got back to her feet. She felt a bit wobbly, but she didn't think she'd be sick again.

"Toast?" Lily asked and received a small smile and nod from Scarlet. "Okay, come on."

It was okay, she could do this. She just needed to

put one foot in front of the other, try to act normally around her housemates, and not blurt out the truth about what a terrible person she was, that she'd let a truly horrible injustice happen today. Her eyes stung, and she rubbed at them, which only made them redder.

Should I tell them? No, I just can't. What would they think of me? Thoughts spun around and around Scarlet's head as she let her housemates look after her. She felt guilty, knowing she wasn't deserving of all this kindness.

Disdain and rejection, that's what I really deserve.

Why are they being so nice? They wouldn't behave this way if they knew the truth. Perhaps I should tell them and let them treat me the way I deserve? Would that make her feel better about the situation? Well, she believed she didn't deserve to feel better about this whole mess, and herself in general. That would be selfish.

Is it selfish to temporarily make myself feel better when people would view me badly in the long run? Perhaps I might lose their friendship and support altogether? That would be the punishment I deserve.

Selfish or not, Scarlet was wary about burning bridges with the girls she lived with. She was tied into a twelve-month contract with the landlord. Moving back home with Marie was an unthinkable situation she didn't think she could bear right now.

The best thing she could think to do was to talk to

Amy. *Will Amy even hear me out?* She wouldn't blame her if she turned her back on her and refused to listen to any explanation Scarlet could give. What would Scarlet do if she were in Amy's position, betrayed by someone she thought was becoming a friend, and with her partner's career and reputation in tatters because of the actions of the person standing in front of her? Would she listen? Could she bear to listen?

Scarlet recognised herself as the villain in Rhys and Amy's story, although she desperately didn't want to be. She wondered what she should have done differently. None of this would've happened if she hadn't misread Rhys' intentions towards her; if she hadn't told her mother about her crush on Rhys; if she'd told Hannah the truth when she took her statement. If she'd stood up to her mother, she could've avoided this whole mess. Why hadn't she been stronger?

Because I've always been weak and malleable. She could practically hear Marie's voice in her head, dripping her usual vitriol into her ear.

Shaking her head, she promised herself she would explain everything to Amy. Even if it meant ruining herself and her mother in the process, she had to make this right.

Chapter Thirty-Six

"Do you have the book on Marx?"

Amy mentally rolled her eyes before replying to the lanky boy who was standing on the other side of the enquiry desk. "Do you know which book you want? There are several."

"Um, the one with the blue cover? I picked it up last week, but I had too many books out on my account so I put it back on the trolley."

"Okay, so you've looked on the shelf where you got it from before, and it's not there?" The student shook his head. "I'm sorry, someone else must've borrowed it. There are lots of other books on Marx, perhaps a different one would be suitable?"

Sometimes Amy wondered whether her customers thought she had the name and cover art of every book in the library stored in her head. These conversations always went the same way; the student or lecturer would look so confused when the librarian wasn't able to magic up a specific book from a sketchy description or wrongly remembered title.

Rhys insisted Amy return to work today. They'd been bouncing around at home, not really knowing how to help each other. It was best for at least one of them to hold on to a shred of normality. It felt good being back at the library, and she was glad to have the distraction. There were only a few weeks left of this term, so the library was busy with students trying to finish assignments due before the Christmas break.

During the two week break, the number of students on campus would fall dramatically and most of the library inhabitants would be faculty trying to catch up on their personal research projects. The librarians would have a bit of breathing room to blitz through some backroom admin tasks that had fallen by the wayside while they focused the students. Normally she would look forward to the Christmas and summer holidays when Rhys would spend a good proportion of her day in the library, tucked away at a desk by the big windows that looked out over The Green. During Amy's breaks, they would people watch out the window and share a steaming cup of coffee — in a lidded container, obviously — Amy was a librarian after all. She had to practise what she preached. At lunchtimes, Rhys would pack up her things, and they'd head to the cafe for food, Peggy following faithfully at Amy's side.

Running her fingers through Peggy's wiry fur, Amy thought about last February when they'd had snow. The Green had been blanketed in white, and Peggy enjoyed bounding through the white powder when they took her outside. The memory made her smile. Sometimes it was the little things in life that brought you happiness. She hoped she could maintain that positive attitude, even with everything that was happening at the moment. It was hard, but she would try, both for Rhys' and for her own sake. Not only did they have Rhys' job to worry about, but Amy was still dreading every letter that fell through the letterbox. She would bend down to retrieve the envelopes from the mat and say a silent prayer to any deity who would listen that there wasn't a letter from the DVLA to say she had to stop driving.

Peggy got one last scratch behind her ear before Amy returned to her work with a heavy heart.

A crowd of students entered the library at the same time as Scarlet. She didn't want to bump into Amy unexpectedly, so she used them as cover to get in without being in full view of the enquiry desks. She didn't really have a plan. She just knew she needed to talk to Amy and try to explain as best she could. That's all she could hope to do at this stage.

With luck she didn't feel she deserved, Scarlet found an empty desk, so she could effectively hide in plain sight among crowds of students. They were all bundled up in coats and scarves, heads down, working on last-minute assignments.

Psyching herself up was unfortunately nothing new to Scarlet. She wondered sometimes at how often she found herself in uncomfortable situations which required her to conjure up some mental fortitude. Was it her fault she ended up in these situations? She liked to think she was in control of her own destiny, that there wasn't some higher power playing with her life. Occasionally she wished she could blame the bad stuff on a malevolent puppet master. That would free her conscience considerably.

Thinking these things made the guilt creep back in. She was solely responsible for all the bad that she'd done and continued to do. Perhaps she could do some tiny thing to make things right. Perhaps it wasn't too late to undo the train wreck her mother had created in her selfish pursuit for money.

The clock on the library wall ticked. The faces of the students around her slowly changed, replaced with new people intent on getting their work finished. A steady hum of whispered conversation accompanied the tap of fingers on keys as people got closer to submitting their assignments, one typed word at a time.

Scarlet had a book open on the desk in front of her, but she wasn't reading it. She'd spotted Amy a couple of times in the last hour, but she hadn't found the courage to approach her yet. Should she wait until Amy's lunch break? Maybe talk to her outside when she took Peggy out for a run on The Green? No, that didn't feel right. It also pigeonholed her into having to act at a specific time, even if she hadn't properly psyched herself up.

Then she saw Amy, Peggy at her side, pushing a trolley of books across the far side of the library. This was the first time Scarlet had seen her without a student or other librarian. It was as good a chance as she was going to get.

Flipping the textbook closed, she got up. Her chair was quickly occupied by a student who'd been circling, on the lookout for a seat. In order to catch up with Amy, she made her way between the milling students as quickly as she could. Amy turned a corner, forcing Scarlet to look down several aisles to find her.

When Amy looked up, Scarlet waved to get her attention. It made her sad to see the smile slip from Amy's face when she realised who it was. She clamped her lips together, shaking her head and holding up a hand to stop Scarlet when she opened her mouth to speak.

"Scarlet," Amy said as her face went pale, "I don't think I should talk to you."

Without a lawyer present.

Reading the panic on Amy's face, Scarlet backed up a couple of steps. The last thing she wanted to do was cause Amy any more upset.

"Please, Amy, I really want to explain this to you."

"Why? To make yourself feel better? No, Scarlet. I won't let you unburden yourself onto me. That's not fair. There's nothing you can say to make this right. Do you even understand what you've done? Rhys is suffering because of your lies."

"I never meant for you to get caught up in all this," Scarlet gesticulated, meaning Marie's plan.

"What? So it was only Rhys you wanted to hurt? No, Scarlet, it doesn't work like that. So many people are being affected by your lies. Not just Rhys, but her department and her colleagues, her family and me! I thought we were friends, Scarlet? Were you just using me to find out personal things about my girlfriend, things you could use against her?"

"Amy, I promise you, I didn't even know she was your girlfriend at first." Amy made a dismissive noise in her throat. "I honestly believed she was interested in me."

"She was friendly and being a supportive teacher. You took that and ran with it until you had, what? Conjured up some fantasy relationship between the two of you? Are you telling me you actually believed there was something real there, not just a malicious accusation to punish the lecturer who's class you were failing?"

Without her realising it, Amy's voice had risen progressively louder as she got more and more upset. They were in a quiet aisle, but Scarlet was aware their conversation was attracting the attention of some nearby eavesdroppers.

She turned and ran, disappearing around the shelves and out of sight, leaving Amy to take a few deep breaths to calm herself. Scarlet had been the last person she'd expected to see.

Chapter Thirty-Seven

"Are you okay, Amy?" Her colleague, Jaheem, asked after seeing the look on Amy's face when she returned the trolley to the enquiry desk.

"It's been a tough week. I just had a bit of an argument with someone who I thought was my friend. But it's okay, she's left now." She smiled weakly at the other librarian. They both knew she wasn't really alright.

"Do you want to take your lunch break now? Get a bit of fresh air with Peggy to clear your head?"

"Thanks for the offer, but I think I'll get this other trolley of books shelved first." The second trolley was sorted for the reference section on the second floor. Amy pushed it into the lift, glad to have something to do to distract her mind from everything that was going on. As the metal doors closed behind her, she scratched Peggy behind the ears thoughtfully, seeking comfort from her furry companion. Rhys had a meeting with the university board this afternoon. She'd offered to take the day off work again to be with her girlfriend, but Rhys insisted she try to get back to her normal routine. Helen was going to keep her daughter company during the morning and then drive her across town for the meeting at two o'clock.

The lift doors opened onto the reference floor, and Amy began working her way down the aisles with the trolley. Like any good librarian, she'd already sorted the books into Dewey order so she could work methodically. It was the most efficient way. As she worked, she found some books that'd been shoved back into the wrong place by harried students, so she tidied as she went, making sure the books would be easy to find for the next person who needed them.

The trolley was half-finished when Peggy started to get agitated. At first, Amy wondered whether she'd forgotten about a planned fire drill, but this wasn't Peggy's usual way of alerting to the fire alarm. Her small dog looked up at her expectantly and turned in a tight circle. "What is it, Peg?"

Peggy turned and looked up at her owner again.

Amy frowned and shook her head, not understanding what her dog was alerting her to. "Show me?"

Peggy yipped and turned to lead her human between the shelves of books. It would have been comical, the way Peggy's tail stood up like an antenna and her wiry little bottom wiggled as she walked. But Amy couldn't laugh at the bossy littler terrier when she had no idea what she was being led towards. It could be anything — a fire? No, she couldn't smell smoke. A fight between a group of students? No, she didn't feel any vibrations through the floor.

Nervousness fluttered through her at not knowing, but she trusted Peggy, who was leading her towards something rather than away from a danger. Soon it became clear that the dog was heading towards the back of the library, where the study pods were. The pods were glass rooms with a large table inside each one, big enough for six to eight students to sit around.

The shelves were packed tightly with books, so Amy couldn't see through to the aisles on either side of her. Only the pod directly in front of her was visible, and she could see it was empty. It wasn't until she came to the end of the shelves that she could see the pods on either side of it. Peggy headed straight for pod number five, which had its number etched onto the glass door.

At first, Amy could only see that a figure was huddled in the corner of the room, but as she reached for the door handle, she recognised Scarlet. She sat on the floor with her legs pulled up to her chest, her hair partly covering the red blotchiness of her face. She didn't look up at the sound of the door opening. Perhaps she was crying too loudly to hear it? Or maybe she was just so caught up in her emotions that she couldn't register what was going on around her.

Once the door was open far enough, Peggy squeezed her wiry little body through and went straight to Scarlet. She pressed against the shaking human and licked the salty tears from her cheeks. Scarlet's arms came up around the dog, and she hugged her, pressing her face into Peggy's neck. Peggy allowed Scarlet to hold her, making soft chuffing noises to soothe the human.

Crossing the room, Amy approached Scarlet cautiously. She didn't want to scare her. Her breathing came hard and fast, indicating Scarlet had been crying for some time. Amy knelt slowly in front of her, worried she was going to hyperventilate and pass out. She called Scarlet's name, quietly at first because she didn't want to startle her. She wanted to make her presence known before she resorted to reaching out and gently touching Scarlet's foot.

To her credit, Scarlet only jumped slightly. Red ringed eyes rose to look at Amy and her lip trembled uncontrollably. She tried to say something, but Amy couldn't lip read what she was trying to say. Shaking her head, she told Scarlet she couldn't understand until she calmed down.

Shaking hands slowly released their grip on Peggy's fur, and Scarlet had to let the blood flow return to them before she clumsily signed *Sorry*.

Gradually Scarlet regained enough control of her

breathing to speak clearly, and Amy asked, "I thought you'd left?"

"I wanted to, that would have been the easy thing to do." She looked up towards the ceiling and a stray tear squeezed out of her eye. "But I know I can't run from my problems like that. It would be selfish. I need to try my best to make things right, and if I can't make them right, then at least I want you to know the truth." Scarlet touched Amy's hand, grateful when she didn't pull away. "No matter what you think of me, Amy, I want to tell you I'm not a selfish person. None of this was my doing, not on purpose at least."

"You're not going to try to convince me this was Rhys' fault, are you?" Amy interrupted. "I know she didn't come onto you, Scarlet. She's not a flirt, and she holds herself to very high standards when it comes to her responsibilities to her students. You *are* one of her students. You're a first-year, so you're. . .what? Eighteen, nineteen? You're half her age."

"That's not uncommon in my mother's circles. Her best friend's late husband was in his seventies, thirty years older than her. But that's besides the point." Scarlet gave a small shrug and a self-deprecating smile, "None of this is Rhys' fault, and I take full responsibility. I read the situation wrong. I had no idea she had a partner, and I'm not used to people caring about me, so I read her friendliness as romantic interest."

"She was just being kind to a student who she could see was struggling."

"I know that now, but by the time I realised it was too late. My mother had taken the idea and run with it, using it to her advantage as usual."

"What do you mean?"

"It was all my mum, that's what I was trying to explain. She pounced on the idea that my teacher had taken advantage of me." She held up a hand to silence Amy's protest. "It's how her mind works. She took something I said and twisted it until it was something gross, and so much bigger than us. I didn't know her full plan until I had a lawyer contact me to draw up a grievance against the university. Mum coached me on what to say. First, she wanted me to seduce Rhys and break you two up. When I refused she wanted me to get some evidence of a fake affair with Rhys, but I couldn't do it." The last of her words came out in a rush.

Amy couldn't keep the shock from her voice. "She has no qualms about involving her daughter in her illegal and immoral games? This is extortion and blackmail we're talking about!"

"I know, I know. And I don't want any part of it!"

"But you did!"

"She told me she would lose the house if I didn't go along with it. Apparently, she put the house up in lieu of a retainer for the lawyer."

"So she was blackmailing you too? Her own daughter?"

"Yeah." Scarlet nodded dejectedly. "It's just how she is, I can't remember a time when she's been any different."

"Do you understand how badly she's been treating you?"

Scarlet shrugged. "I always thought that's how parents were with their kids."

"No, I promise you it isn't." Amy sighed. "Listen, I won't pretend I'm not still really angry with you, Scarlet."

"You have every right to be," Scarlet agreed in a small voice. "I deserve it."

"But now that you've told me, we can do something about it. This isn't going to be easy on you."

"I know." Scarlet nodded. "This has been eating away at me for days; my conscience is damned if I do and damned if I don't. I don't know how I ended up in such an awful situation, Amy. I mean, I never thought my mum could do something so evil, so self-centred, so money-grabbing. She's always been *unique* but never quite like this."

Amy nodded for her to continue.

"I wanted to tell the lawyer to retract my statement. To hell with mum and the house! I wanted to make things right for Rhys, and you."

"Why didn't you do that?"

Taking a deep breath, Scarlet fortified herself to answer. "There's something else that's been going on over the last few days. I accidentally uncovered a massive secret, now mum's forbidden me to contact the legal assistant who is handling the case. She asked me out."

"Really?" Amy raised both eyebrows in surprise.

"But mum found out about it and blurted out that she's my sister, well, half-sister."

"Woah." Amy blinked, making a gesture that even a sign language novice could interpret as surprise. "Right, well, that was the last thing I was expecting you to say. You didn't know you had a half-sister, I take it?" Scarlet shook her head in reply.

"That must've been a big shock for you. That's definitely something for us to unpack later. First, let's worry about the more time-sensitive issue — Rhys' meeting with the university board is starting about now."

"We should go, I can talk to them. Tell them what really happened."

"Thank you, Scarlet. You know this is going to have ramifications for your degree, don't you?"

"Yes, I know. But to be honest with you, I feel like it's been slipping through my fingers since I got here, anyway. I'm not sure I'm really cut out for this, after all. Perhaps it's for the best I stop trying to flog a dead horse and admit this wasn't the right thing for me."

"Do you have any idea what you'd like to do

instead?" Amy asked as she climbed to her feet and held out her hand. Scarlet gave Peggy one last scratch behind the ears before letting Amy pull her to her feet.

"Well—oh—it'll sound silly to you."

"No, go on, tell me," Amy encouraged as they made their way around the table and out of the study pod.

"I've really been enjoying learning sign language, and I seem to have a good memory for it. I thought I might look into doing a qualification."

"That's a fantastic idea." Amy turned and grabbed her wrist. "Now, I'm sorry, but I can't walk backwards to read your lips all the way across campus, so can we talk more about this later?"

They rushed through the library with Peggy trotting at their side, only making a quick stop so Amy could tell Jaheem she was taking her lunch break and that she might be back late. Then they jogged out the main doors and made their way along the winding paths that crossed the campus to the administration building. Without realising it, both women had the same thought in mind. *Please don't let us be too late.*

Chapter Thirty-Eight

The chairs weren't any more comfortable than Rhys remembered as she sat with her mum in the lobby of the admin building. She bent forward with her elbows on her knees, hands clasped together. White knuckles told Helen how her daughter was feeling without the need for words. Leaning over, she rubbed Rhys' arm in silent support. Trying to be the strong one was tough when all of her maternal instincts were screaming inside her to protect her daughter from this awful thing. *I'd give anything to make this better, ease her pain.*

Each time they heard a door opening or footsteps coming down the corridor, they both looked up, at the same time not wanting the meeting to start, but equally needing to get it over with.

In an unusual show of defiance, the sun managed to break through the grey of the winter sky and shine down on Scarlet and Amy as they jogged along in the cold air. Scarlet lifted her face upwards and tried to soak up the little warmth it offered. The weather had been horrible for the last week. She took the sun's appearance as a sign she was choosing to do the right thing.

This is good. This is positive. She was confident in her decision to break away from the oppressive cloud of her mother's control. A smile touched her lips. *I am a good person; I'm making a conscious choice to be better.*

The smartwatch on Amy's wrist vibrated to tell her a new hour had started. It was two o'clock, and Rhys' meeting should be starting now. That was, if the board didn't try to play mind games and keep her waiting. Picking up speed, she called out to Scarlet, turning slightly to see if her friend replied. In turning her body to be able to see Scarlet's lips, Amy changed direction slightly and accidentally collided with Peggy, who was too close to adjust to Amy in time to avoid her feet.

Peggy yelped. Amy tumbled and went sprawling over top of the terrier, landing on her hands and knees on the path.

"Amy!" Scarlet shouted automatically, even though Peggy was the only one who could hear her. Once Scarlet helped Amy back to her feet, they both fussed over Peggy to make sure she was alright. She yipped but seemed otherwise okay.

———

"The board is ready for you now, Dr Hunter." Rhys and Helen exchanged a look at Linda's icy tone.

"Whatever happened to innocent until proven guilty?" Helen muttered under her breath, earning her a tight-lipped smile from her daughter, which didn't meet her eyes.

"That's Linda, Dr Khatri's secretary; she's not my biggest fan at the best of times. I'm sure she's loving all this."

"Are you sure you don't want me to come in with you, sweetheart?"

"No, mum, I—"

"Now, Dr Hunter," Linda barked.

Rhys glared across the lobby at the uppity woman before turning back to her mum.

"No, I don't want you to hear the horrible lies they're going to spout about me in there. There's no need to put you through that. That's why I didn't want Amy here either. I'm sure they're going to say some things you wouldn't be able to un-hear."

"Okay, if it will really make you feel better."

"It will, thanks, mum. And thank you for being here."

"Of course. That's what mothers are for."

"Love you, mum."

"I love you too, Rhys."

Crossing the lobby felt like crossing a frozen desert to Rhys. She felt each step taking her further away from the love and warmth of her family and towards the barren desolation of the conference room, filled with people who were about to rip her life away from her.

As she reached the doorway, Paul joined her, and she trudged in after him. The door slammed shut behind them.

A blast of hot, dry air hit Scarlet and Amy when the lobby doors slid open. Helen stood to greet them. "Amy, love, we weren't expecting you. I thought you were going to meet us at home once you finished work? Rhys didn't want me to go in with her; she said it would be too hard to listen to."

"I know; that's why she wanted me at work today. She said it was so I could get back to some normality, but I knew deep down she didn't want me to know exactly what they said about her."

"That's what she told me too. Even in all this mess she's trying to protect us." Helen squeezed Amy's hand, showing a deep sense of love for her. "She loves you so much, Amy. I'm so glad you have each other."

Keeping hold of Amy's hand, Helen tried to move to seat Amy and the girl with her in the cluster of chairs she'd vacated. She felt the resistance before Amy said, "Helen, this is Scarlet."

"Hello, dear." Helen smiled before registering the name of the girl she was being introduced to. She looked at Amy, then back to Scarlet, frowning. "Um, Scarlet as in. . .?" She gestured towards the double doors across the lobby where Rhys' meeting was currently taking place.

"Yes." Amy held out both of her hands in supplication. "But listen, Scarlet's explained to me what's happened. Her mum's made all this up to extort money out of the university. Scarlet's been painted as the villain in all this, but it's not her fault, she's a victim, too."

Helen pressed her hand to her chest, shock clear on her face."Well, that is quite something."

"I need to get in there and talk to them," Scarlet said, speaking for the first time.

"You're going to have to get past Mrs Snootipants over there," Helen said, tossing her head towards the stern-looking woman guarding the door.

"Pardon?" Amy shook her head, not understanding what Helen just said.

Scarlet tapped Amy's arm. When she had her attention, she fingerspelled "Snootipants".

"I'm sorry, dear. I meant the secretary. She's not very nice."

"Ahh, that's Linda. She doesn't like Rhys because her son also applied for the Head of Psychology position, and Rhys pipped him at the interview. She's held a grudge ever since."

Helen cut her eyes towards Linda. "Do you think she's something to do with all this?"

"No," Scarlet replied. "This is solely my mother's fault. I'm so sorry she's involved your family in her scheme, Mrs Hunter. I want to make it right."

Squaring her shoulders, Scarlet made her way towards the conference room. A few yards away, Linda was about to step in front of the doors to block Scarlet's path. The expression on her face told anyone who cared to look that she was on a mission to ensure the meeting was not disturbed. Instead, the door opened and Hannah walked out behind a woman who Scarlet assumed was Hannah's boss, Pamela Ng.

Scarlet was shocked to see Hannah and whipped around to look at Amy with an almost comical expression on her face. She quickly signed the word "sister." Amy gave her a nod of understanding. It was enough to refocus her, and she used the distraction to dart around Linda and into the room. She heard Hannah call out her name, but the roaring in her ears made her voice sound far away.

Most of the room's occupants were still seated around the table. Her mother's legal team must've completed their part of the meeting and were leaving to allow the board to deal with their wayward employee. Rhys looked up at the commotion by the door. Even from across the room Scarlet could tell Rhys was exhausted. Her eyes, which met Scarlet's, looked almost haunted. "Scarlet? What are you doing here?"

"Dr Hunter, I want to explain."

"I think this is going to take quite a bit of explaining, don't you?" Dr Khatri cut in. He'd immediately picked up on Scarlet's name and realised who'd just barged into this meeting.

"I think the question is, Scarlet, have you come to offer some made-up piece of evidence to get me into even more trouble with your lies?" Rhys shook her head and looked away.

"Hello, Miss Robbins. I'm Dr Khatri, Dean of Dalesbury University. We weren't expecting you to attend this meeting in person. Your legal team read your statement on your behalf."

"They're not *my* legal team," Scarlet said, making sure to stress the word *my,* "They were instructed by my mother. I believe her intention was to fabricate evidence to force the university to pay for her silence, ruining Dr Hunter's reputation in the process."

"You're saying Dr Hunter is just collateral damage in a scheme for money?"

"Unfortunately, yes, Dr Khatri, she is."

"Why should we believe you?" An elderly man, who sat at the table, spoke up.

"Pardon?" Scarlet and Rhys said at the same time, each looking as confused as the other.

"Well," he continued, "If we are to believe that Dr Hunter preyed on this poor girl and coaxed her into some kind of sick affair, then why couldn't it be that Dr Hunter has now threatened her in some way to get her to retract her accusations?"

He leaned back in his chair, a smug expression on his face. It was obvious to everyone else in the room he didn't like Rhys. "Bloody gays, shoving their lifestyles down our throats. It's disgusting."

"That's enough, Bert." A slightly younger man with a thick crop of sliver hair stood and glared at the homophobic board member, "That comment goes against our Diversity and Inclusion policy, and you shouldn't be on the board if you hold those outdated views."

Bert huffed and glared back, folding his thick arms across his chest.

"We're not here to discuss my place on this board; we're here to sack this. . .woman." He ground out the word "woman" like it tasted bad in his mouth.

The silver-haired man looked very familiar to Scarlet, but she couldn't quite place where she knew him from. She watched him while he berated the horrible man — Bert. A couple of the other board members were shaking their heads at him too. "This must be embarrassing for you, Bert, to be called out like this in front of your fellows. I doubt that any of us will be able to muster much respect for you in the future. But thank you; your outburst has taken the decision out of our hands. We will convene another meeting of the board to arrange for you to step down."

Bert heaved himself up to leave and slammed his hand down on the table in anger. As he pushed his chair back, he knocked the table with enough force to tip over a coffee cup. The dark liquid ran towards a pile of Dalesbury University headed paper in front of the silver-haired man, and he moved to snatch it up before it was ruined. His shirt sleeve wasn't so lucky as he scooped up the paper. The coffee managed to soak into the cuff, staining it a muddy brown.

Scarlet stared, her eyes narrowing in on the wet brown stain on his white shirt. His name was on the tip of her tongue, something she hadn't remembered in a long time. Suddenly she was a little girl, sitting in the bay window, digging her nails into the rubber seal to leave the satisfying little crescent moon indents.

A white shirt stained brown. Not with coffee, but with mud.

In a tiny little-girl voice, so quiet almost no one heard her, Scarlet whispered, "Brian?"

The man snapped his head towards her at the sound of his own name.

Chapter Thirty-Nine

"Brian? It is you, isn't it?" Scarlet tilted her head to the side to study the man in amazement. "Do you remember me? I must have been about six the last time you saw me."

He turned around, taking his time to study her face, "You're Marie's daughter. Of course I remember you. Your surname has changed, so I didn't make the connection before now. But wow, look at you Scarlet, you're a young lady now!"

Dr Khatri cleared his throat loudly. "Can we return to the matter at hand? You obviously felt you had something to add, Miss Robbins, so speak."

"Yes! Yes, please." Scarlet physically and mentally scrambled to address the board. It felt like a weight was being lifted off her shoulders as she told them about what her mother had done.

When she finished, the female board member wrinkled her brow and said, "I hate to agree with Bert, but this sounds preposterous. It's like a Brothers Grimm story."

Dr Khatri nodded in agreement, "We've seen the photos from your phone, Scarlet. And the messages."

"What photos and messages?"

"Your legal team submitted photos of you and Dr Hunter embracing, and messages between the two of you which clearly suggest a sexual relationship."

"No, that's not possible. Let me see them?"

As he was still standing, Brian reached for the stack of papers on the table and shuffled through them until he found the ones he was looking for. He passed them to Scarlet, who looked at them, shaking her head slowly.

"I didn't send these messages. It looks like they've come from my account, but perhaps mum got hold of my phone. She's not that tech savvy, but she knows how to take a screenshot and delete a message thread."

"What about the pictures?" Dr Khatri asked, "Do you deny that's you and Dr Hunter in the photo?"

"No, but—"

"I'm not sure we can just take your word for this, Miss Robbins; it's gone too far."

"What?" Rhys stood up from her chair. "She's telling you she lied, and now that she's telling the truth you're not going to believe her?"

"Dr Hunter, please sit down."

"No, I won't sit quietly and let you brush me and my career aside so you can protect the university's reputation. Scarlet is recanting her accusation, for goodness' sake! What more will it take to make you see what's happening here?"

With a frustrated breath, Scarlet turned to Brian. "You remember what mum was like all those years ago, don't you Brian?"

He gave a slow nod and motioned for her to continue. "Well, she's ten times worse now. She's been drinking more and more. I've been trying to manage her finances, but I think she's hiding debt from me, moving it from one credit card to another. She crashed her car," she said, cutting a look to Rhys, "and she was probably drinking, I know I shouldn't think badly of my mother, but I just know the crash was her fault. She could have really hurt Amy and Peggy. It would have been my fault for not doing something about her sooner!"

Rhys looked confused. "What do you mean? The car accident. . .that was your mother? Did she target Amy's car on purpose?"

Rhys clenched her hands into fists in anger, feeling a fierce protectiveness for her girlfriend.

"No." Scarlet held out her hands to calm Rhys down. "I don't have any reason to think she even knew she'd met you and Amy until I mentioned Peggy's name recently. It was a big coincidence. She kept it from me, I only found out she'd had an accident when she let it slip last week."

"She tried to blackmail Amy into paying cash for the repairs to her Audi when it was Amy's car that came off worse."

"Blackmail? How?"

"She told Amy, and I quote, 'disabled girls like her shouldn't be driving' and she was going to report Amy to the DVLA if she didn't pay up."

"That's awful." Scarlet's voice softened and she said, "and unfortunately, sounds exactly like my mother."

"Amy is terrified of losing her independence. Being able to drive means so much to her."

"I'm so sorry, Rhys. I feel like this is my fault for not intervening with mum sooner."

"She's the parent, Scarlet, not you. She shouldn't be your responsibility."

Brian reached out and patted Scarlet's shoulder. When she looked up and met his eyes, she saw he understood. He had lived with Marie for several years, after all.

She asked in a small voice, "You believe me, don't you, Brian?"

"Yes, I believe your mother is capable of all the things you've said. Try not to worry. I'm going to help you sort this out."

"I knew there was a reason you were my favourite stepdad," Scarlet said jokingly. Brian responded with a sad smile that told her he understood what she had gone through in the twelve years since he'd driven off down that driveway.

"I'm sorry that I had to leave you with her, Scarlet."

"I know you didn't have a choice. Recently I've realised mum has been gaslighting me and many other people for a long time. She's been the puppet master, pulling all of our strings, making us perform her malevolent dance. I recognise it now, and I can't let her go on hurting people I care about, Rhys, Amy, and you, Brian —even though it was years ago."

Brian smiled encouragingly at her. "And what about you, Scarlet? You can't let her hurt *you* anymore either."

Out in the lobby of the admin building, Amy watched as Hannah and the well-dressed woman who must be Hannah's boss stared at the closed door. They stood close, probably hoping to hear what was going on inside. At first, Amy thought Linda was going to hustle them away but the nosy secretary seemed to debate for a moment and then moved to eavesdrop at the door too.

Amy leaned closer to Helen and whispered in her ear, "That woman over there, the younger one? She's Scarlet's half-sister, only she doesn't know it."

Helen turned so Amy could read her lips and

mouthed silently, "Wow, she looks. . .expensive. They're the lawyers?"

"Yeah."

Pamela had heard enough. That Marie woman had taken them for a ride, and her blood boiled with embarrassment. They were a well-respected firm, infamous in their field. They didn't get played with like the puppets in some dodgy legal game.

Grabbing Hannah by the elbow, Pamela hurried them both away from the conference room and across the lobby. The blast of chilled air hit them at the same time as they stepped outside. The last of the winter sun's rays were about to dip below the rooftops as the afternoon wore on.

"What the hell just happened in there?"

"I don't know, I'm as shocked as you are, Pamela."

"I sent you to take that girl's statement because I thought she would open up more to someone closer to her own age. You're not an intern or a PA; I expect my legal assistant to be able to tell when a client is giving a statement under duress."

"She seemed genuinely upset."

"You were too busy thinking with your libido to realise she was spinning a pack of lies to your face," Pamela spat. "I hope she was a good fuck, Hannah. I hope it was worth it, because you no longer work for me. Get your daddy to hook you up with another job. I shouldn't have to remind you we don't sleep with our clients."

Sleep with our clients. Hannah mulled that thought over in her head, an idea slowly forming. She tossed a smirk at Pamela. "Thanks for the business advice."

Walking away from her former boss, Hannah spun on her heel for one last parting shot, "You did the initial video consultation with Scarlet's mother, didn't you? And yet, you weren't able to tell that she was orchestrating that pack of lies? At least I can say I was distracted by a pretty damsel in distress, what's your excuse?"

She strolled away before Pamela could reply.

Chapter Forty

"What happened to your hands?" Rhys signed as she walked over to where Amy and her mum were sitting.

"Oh," Amy stared down at her scuffed palms. "I tripped over Peg, and put my hands out to break my fall."

"It's a good job they're only grazed, and you didn't break your wrist. You'd have a hard time helping me learn sign language with one arm in a cast, wouldn't you?" Scarlet smiled good-naturedly as she joined in the conversation.

Helen stood up as she asked her daughter, "Is it over, sweetheart?"

"Yes." Rhys squeezed her mum while keeping her face turned towards Amy, "Brian used to know Scarlet's mother, and he convinced the other board members she was malicious enough to be capable of this whole thing."

Amy nodded and closed her eyes, taking a deep breath of relief. The chair next to her sent out the vibrations of movement. She knew that Rhys had sat down with her. She opened her eyes and looked into her girlfriend's relieved face. "Amy, you are one incredible woman. I don't want to think how this might've turned out. What if you hadn't brought Scarlet over here? Our entire lives could've been destroyed today. You had the strength of character to see what she had to say, where someone else might've ignored her." She pulled Amy's hands into her lap. "You don't need my validation, but thank you."

Then they were kissing and smiling and crying all at the same time.

The relief crackled around them.

This time, witnessing Rhys kiss Amy made Scarlet smile. She realised she felt genuinely happy for them, and also for Helen, who simultaneously hugged her and thanked her.

As he walked past their group, Dr Khatri told Scarlet, "We will need to hold another meeting, Miss Robbins, to discuss your future at Dalesbury."

Turning in Helen's arms, Scarlet nodded."Okay, Dr Khatri."

"Oh no, I'm sorry, love," Helen said, giving her an extra squeeze.

"No, it's really okay. I'm gonna go in a different direction. I'm going to leave uni and do a BSL qualification instead. Amy said she'd give me a hand."

"That'll be a really positive move for you, Scarlet." Rhys said, "You've made such good progress in our signing lessons. You've got a good memory for it."

Beaming, Scarlet felt herself relax for the first time in weeks. The praise felt nice. Coming from Rhys, it gave Scarlet confidence that perhaps she might eventually be forgiven. She realised the excited feeling that spiked inside her when she thought about Rhys was gone. Now, she just felt proud of herself for something she'd done, just her. She settled back in her chair and allowed Rhys to fill Amy and Helen in on what had happened, including the revelation it had been Marie who crashed into Amy's car.

Eventually Amy peeled herself out of Rhys' lap and made her way back to the library with Peggy. She could focus on her work again now two of her worries had been lifted. She promised to meet up with Scarlet the following day to help her find a good BSL course to enrol on. There should be several starting in January, and hopefully there'd still be space for Scarlet.

They arranged for Helen to drive Rhys home, and Amy would meet her there after she finished the rest of the afternoon at work. Helen had suggested they come for dinner at her house, but Amy had given Rhys a look that said she wanted them to be in their own home tonight. Rhys had nodded her agreement and made arrangements to see her parents over the weekend.

The house was quiet when Scarlet let herself in. Her housemates were likely still over on campus, either in seminars or working in the library.

Thinking about the library made her think of Amy, and Scarlet felt relief wash over her again. Her friends were free from their turmoil, and now she needed to work on her own. First, she would talk to her house-mates, tell them everything, and throw herself on their mercy. Then she would work out what to do with her mother. She was under no illusion that now was the time to do something about Marie once and for all. If only she could work out what that something was.

Half an hour later the front door opened and the burr of several voices floated down the hall and into the kitchen where Scarlet waited. The oven was on, heating the room nicely. Scarlet had cooked pizza for her friends, and she put a bowl of salad in the middle of the table as they came in.

"What's all this?" Jessica asked as she swiped a tomato from the bowl and popped it into her mouth.

"I was hoping I could talk to you all? So I made pizza!" She forced cheer into her voice as she motioned at the table set for four. She wobbled and said in a smaller voice, "Will you sit with me?"

The other three girls didn't have to be asked twice. They each pulled out a chair and sat down as Scarlet took two large pizzas from the oven and sliced them.

Taking a deep breath, she piled the slices of pizza onto a big plate and carried it to the table. She sat in the last chair, and as the others dug into the food, she told them everything.

"So the hot lawyer chick turned out to be your sister?" Lily said as she crammed her last piece of pizza into her mouth.

"She's not technically a lawyer, but, um, yeah." Scarlet toyed with the single slice of pizza on her plate. It had long gone cold.

"And she's a Hoffman, of like, *The* Hoffmans?" Jessica added.

"Oh, Allah, if she hadn't turned out to be your sister you could've been set for life with that one." Kemi sighed dreamily. "You said your mum wanted you to find a Sugar Mama, right?"

It was hard for Scarlet to believe she was sitting here with her housemates, *my friends*, she reminded herself. They were still her friends. They were being supportive and joking with her. They'd believed her and wanted to help her.

"You know what?" Jessica pushed her pizza crusts to one side of her plate. "Hannah knows the law, ask her for advice on what to do about your mum."

Nodding thoughtfully, Scarlet rolled the idea around in her mind. Hannah was her best bet for working out what to do with Marie. The problem was, she didn't think there was much legal recourse for what Marie had done. This wasn't the litigious culture of the United States, where Rhys could have counter sued Marie for slander. The car crash was too long ago to prove Marie had been drinking. It would be Amy and Rhys' word against hers. Scarlet needed a different solution to the problem that was her mother.

Lily was a bit quiet, but it wasn't disgust that Scarlet saw in her eyes; it looked like sadness. Later, as they walked up the second flight of stairs to their bedrooms, Scarlet bumped her shoulder against Lily's and asked her why she'd been so quiet.

"I'm just feeling a bit sad you didn't think you could confide in me, in us. I understand why you thought you couldn't say anything, but I just want you to know we *are* your friends Scarlet."

"I'm sorry I didn't tell you all about this sooner. I really believed this was all my fault, that I was this horrible person. That's what my mother made me believe."

"No one should make you feel like that. If only you'd spoken out about how she treated you before, we could've helped you see how misguided that belief was."

"I don't know what I did to deserve friends like you."

"Just keep being you, Scarlet. You have a good heart. You're strong; you haven't let your mum's personality poison you."

"Thanks, Lil. I know I should feel angry with her, and I do, but mostly I just feel overwhelmingly sad."

"I know, babes, and you are perfectly justified in feeling like that. Whatever feelings you're having are valid, remember that, okay?"

Scarlet sniffled in response.

"Try to get some sleep; you've had a stressful few days. Today was massive. You can sleep easy knowing you did the right thing and stopped an innocent woman losing her job. I know you're still worried about what to do about your mum, but you're on the home stretch now. It's gonna be okay."

"I know. After everything that's happened, I've realised I need more help with her than I can do myself."

They hugged at the top of the stairs and went into their bedrooms on opposite sides of the landing.

Chapter Forty-One

Peggy was worn out after her walk. Rhys sat on the sofa with Amy curled against her. They'd ordered their favourite Chinese food and watched a documentary about a murderer on TV. The stress of the last few days melted away, and they could finally relax.

Amy tugged on Rhys' arm. "Let's go to bed, Ree."

"Are you tired, darling?"

"No." She drew out the word seductively. "But I thought, perhaps, I could help take your mind off everything that's been happening. Like you helped me after the car accident."

"So, it's got nothing to do you being a horny little minx?"

"Are you too full of Chinese food to have sex with me?"

Rhys burst out laughing and pulled Amy onto her

lap. She kissed her, the sort of joyous open-mouthed kiss that was all teeth, and love, and smiles. "I love you so much, Amy."

The bedroom was dark until Amy turned on the lamp. It threw the room into a golden glow as she led her girlfriend by the hand towards their bed. They stood close, slowly undressing each other. There was never a moment when they weren't touching as they undid buttons and pulled down zips. Mouths brushed skin and fingers lingered over lips as they spoke to each other with their bodies.

With the light on, Amy could read Rhys' body language as well as her words. Making love like this was an experience Rhys thanked Amy for every day. Before being with her, a lover who used sight and touch to make up for another of her senses, Rhys'd had enjoyable sex, but no one compared to Amy.

Two piles of clothes pooled on the floor and two nude women slid under the covers. They spooned, with Amy's back pressed to Rhys' chest. Right now Amy didn't need to see Rhys' lips because she could feel what they were doing as they kissed along the back of her shoulder. She ground her bottom back into Rhys and felt the vibration of the growl that came from her mouth. The hand that landed on her hip was firm yet tender as it pulled her back more solidly. That same hand stroked down to her knee and levered it upwards, parting her legs.

Amy sighed in pleasure when fingers dipped between her thighs. She twisted the top half of her body around so they could kiss. Their mouths met slowly, matching the pace of Rhys' hand. Wetness spread over Amy's clit and she groaned at the feeling of the hood being rubbed back and forth. Her entrance tingled with wanting, needing Rhys' fingers to travel lower. She reached down and took Rhys' hand, moving it to where she needed her. Lips smiled against the skin of Amy's shoulder as Rhys pushed her fingers inside slowly and deeply. This was truly what bliss felt like, for both of them.

They rocked together, mutually setting a steady pace. A hand skidded back over Rhys' side, her skin goose-bumped where Amy's fingers touched her. Then Amy's hand was sliding between their bodies, finding Rhys' clit and circling it. Each time Amy's hips rocked back, her bottom pushed her hand harder against Rhys.

They continued to kiss, Amy twisting backwards while Rhys propped herself up on her elbow to lean over Amy. As the pulse of their bodies picked up, it became harder and harder to keep the kiss gentle and tender. They pressed their lips together harder, tongues caressing and teeth nipping. Amy hummed a jubilant vibration into Rhys' mouth, a sure sign that her orgasm was approaching. Feeling Rhys' fingers curl just a little bit more inside her to press hard on her g-spot, Amy's muscles clamped down. Heat raced through her body, starting in her core and radiating outwards. She dropped her head back onto Rhys' shoulder, momentarily pausing the motion of her hand as her body relaxed involuntarily.

"Ree," she breathed, raising her head to look at Rhys' face in the mirror on the wardrobe door. "I love you. I know it's a cliche to say it just after you've made me come, but it's just as true in this moment as it is when you're arguing with me about what to watch on TV or when you're picking up after Peggy. I love you."

Their eye contact in the mirror was full of love, and Rhys felt her heart swell with feeling for this amazing woman she had the privilege to hold in her arms. "I love you too."

"Good. Now get up here and sit on my face; I want to watch you while you come." Turning onto her back, she motioned for Rhys to straddle her.

She crawled up Amy's body, so she was kneeling over her shoulders. This position had several advantages. Not only could Rhys hold on to the headboard for support, but it allowed Amy a clear line of sight up her girlfriend's body. She really loved to watch every twitch and shudder as she worked her magic on her with her tongue.

Soft golden light caressed Rhys' torso. Her skin glowed and a fine sheen of sweat broke out as her movements picked up speed, encouraged by Amy's hands on her hips.

That perfect, smooth, wet muscle worked her relentlessly, driving her closer and closer towards what she knew was going to be a shattering climax. Amy gave most of her focus to Rhys' clit, but every so often she would sweep her tongue down around her opening and collect the sweet yet tangy liquid that her ministrations were producing.

Rhys gritted her teeth as she came, riding Amy's mouth, her legs shaking with the effort to hold herself up. A renewed flood of wetness escaped from her centre and she knew she'd just soaked Amy's chin, possibly her neck too.

"Sorry," she signed sheepishly to Amy, whose eyes twinkled up at her from between her legs. "I'm not trying to drown you, I promise."

Rhys moved off her once she could unlock her knees and went to fetch a towel. Amy ran her hand down her own neck, tracing the wetness where it had pooled in the hollow of her throat. She laughed and brought her fingers to her mouth. "Wow, you really needed that, huh? And you never, ever, have to be sorry for an orgasm, especially one as powerful as that."

As Amy sat up, Rhys watched, mesmerised, as her own juices trailed down the skin of her girlfriend's chest and between her breasts.

God bless gravity, she thought as she licked her lips and tossed the towel aside, forgotten. Her tongue would do a much better job of cleaning her girlfriend up. Amy registered the gleam in Rhys'eye just before she pounced to press her back onto the bed again. She put her hand out, palm on Rhys' chest, to stop her. "Rhys, will you marry me?"

Later, they lay face-to-face. Their kisses tasted of each other, of love, and sex, and perfection.

Chapter Forty-Two

The streets bustled with people doing their Christmas shopping. With only a few weeks left to get their presents bought and wrapped, they obviously felt the press of time as they converged on the shops.

Marie pulled her collar up higher against the chill and tucked her hand into the crook of Greg's elbow. A modest number of high end shopping bags swung from her other arm. *It's easy enough to convince him to splash out on some pre-holiday luxuries. Now I just need him to give me the best Christmas gift of all: a proposal.*

They took a break from the busy shops and found a wine bar. Instrumental festive music played through hidden speakers as the waiter showed them to the last available table. As Marie sat, she caught sight of a head of silver hair over Greg's shoulder. Slowly she made eye contact with a man she hadn't seen for years.

"Hello, Marie."

Brian. Just what I need.

"I hope Scarlet's okay?" Brain cut his gaze to the back of Greg's head. "After all the trouble you caused for her at the university, I'm surprised to see you in town. I would have thought you'd convince your latest mark to take you on a long holiday until things cooled down."

Greg twisted in his chair and asked, "Marie? What is this?"

"Take my advice." Brian stood and patted Greg on the shoulder. "From someone who knows—cut your losses. Cut all ties with this woman before she really gets her claws into you. She will bleed you dry if she gets the chance. She's well on her way to doing it to her own daughter."

"Brian, how dare you!" Marie exclaimed.

"You don't like being called out on it do you, Marie? But you've always been the organ grinder, making Scarlet dance for your own gains." Brian put some money down on his table and walked away, leaving a spluttering Marie to attempt to pick up the pieces with Greg.

On the other side of town, Scarlet looked out of the large glass window at the crowds, glad she wasn't outside. The independent cafe had been her choice of meeting place, but the hopes it would be quieter than a chain coffee shop were dashed by the massive influx of Christmas shoppers. She'd wanted somewhere reasonably quiet to meet up with Hannah. Yet she also wanted somewhere busy enough to put Hannah off causing a scene.

Her luck had been in as she turned from the counter with her steaming mug, just as the occupants of the table by the window got up to leave. She hoped that was a good omen for the talk she needed to have with Hannah.

My sister, Hannah.

It was still unbelievable that at nineteen she suddenly had siblings she'd known nothing about.

There was a charming *ding* each time the front door opened. It heralded each new customer as they brought a blast of chilly air in with them. It meant Scarlet didn't miss Hannah's arrival, even though her mind wandered as she waited.

A luxurious woolly scarf plopped down onto the table. Like the big wristwatch she'd notice the first time they met, Scarlet noted that the scarf looked very expensive. She also noted Hannah didn't bat an eye when it landed amongst previous customers' coffee rings and cake crumbs.

"Shall I get you another drink?" Hannah asked, looking down into Scarlet's nearly empty mug.

"Um, sure. Thanks. A praline latte, please."

"Coming right up."

As soon as Hannah turned towards the counter, Scarlet scooped up the discarded scarf to shake off the crumbs and frantically wiped at the stained table where it had been. She quickly dropped it back into place when Hannah half turned to smile at her.

"Why so formal, Scarlet?" Hannah looked in puzzlement at the hand Scarlet tucked back against her chest when she'd reached across the table.

"I was actually hoping to pick your brain about a legal question about my mother."

"Oh? Well, I don't work for Pamela anymore." Hannah leaned back in her chair and stuffed her hands into the pockets of her espresso coloured leather jacket. "She fired me because she thought I was sleeping with you." She canted her head, looking intently across the table. "She thought that was why I didn't realise you lied on your statement."

"I'm sorry," Scarlet gasped. "Now I've caused *you* to lose your job! Everything I touch seems to crumble." *This isn't going how I hoped at all. I seem doomed to cost someone their job.*

"No, it's fine. Being a legal assistant wasn't my dream job anyway, and something Pamela said gave me an idea for a business."

"Well, that's something I guess." Her tone didn't sound convinced.

"You know what, Scarlet?" Her gaze turned seductive. "You're not a client anymore. How about we make plans to go on a proper date?"

"Um," Scarlet bit her lip, her cheeks turning as red as her name. "I don't really know how to tell you this, Hannah."

"You're already seeing someone?"

"No, that's not it at all. I wish that was the reason."

"Then what is it? I feel a connection between us, like something is drawing us together."

"Yes," Scarlet nodded. "And I hope we can become good friends, but I'm not sure you'll want to keep in touch with me after I tell you what I found out from my mother. Have you heard of the Westermarck effect?"

Hannah frowned at what seemed like a complete change in subject. "It doesn't ring a bell. What is it?"

"It's the phenomenon that siblings raised together in their early years don't become sexually attracted to one another, but siblings raised apart can if they meet later in life."

"What's that got to do with—"

"Your dad is Christopher Hoffman?" Scarlet cut Hannah off before she could finish her question.

"Yeah, despite trying to distance myself from my dad's side of the family, I don't make a secret of it. What's that got to do with anything?" She leaned forward in her chair as a noisy group of shoppers entered the cafe.

"Because mum spilled the beans to me a few days ago. He's my dad, too."

Eyes wide and mouth open comically, Hannah stared at Scarlet. She opened and closed her mouth several times as if she was going to say something, but the words didn't come.

Scarlet waited patiently until *her sister* was able to form words again. "You're sure this isn't just more of her lies?"

"Unfortunately, I think this time she's telling the truth. She showed me the account where the monthly stipend, or hush money, has been paid into for the last nineteen years. It comes from Hoffman and Sons."

"Well, shit." Hannah slumped back in her chair. Scarlet gave her a minute with her own thoughts before saying, "Just another one of the many coincidences that have been happening in my life recently."

She shrugged dejectedly, "You don't even know the half of what's been going on."

"Tell me?"

Scarlet explained everything to Hannah. The gaslighting, the childhood bullying, the alcohol. All the men her mother coerced into parting with their money.

The hidden debts and unpaid bills. How Marie had threatened to report Amy to the DVLA so they wouldn't work out that her car insurance had lapsed. How the plan to extort compensation from the university was just the tip of the iceberg.

"So as you can see, I need to stage an intervention."

Hannah raised an eyebrow at her from across the table, "I don't know how I could've helped you as a legal assistant, but as a sister I think there probably is something I can do."

"Really?"

"Well, you know I'm a Hoffman?"

"Yes." Scarlet scrunched her forehead in confusion.

"And you know Hoffman and Sons is a global conglomerate?"

Scarlet nodded slowly.

"So, I'm"—she emphasised the word *I'm*—"Pretty fucking loaded." Scarlet just stared at her.

"Welcome to the family." Hannah paused, "And in grand Hoffman tradition, may I suggest we throw money at the problem?"

"What do you mean?"

"I mean, my dear sister, let me pay to have Marie looked after by the finest jailers money can buy. Perhaps she'll get the help she needs."

Not quite catching Hannah's drift, Scarlet's forehead knitted. "I'm sorry, I'm not following you."

"The Priory!" Hannah held out her hands.

"Rehab? I don't think she'll agree to that."

"The most luxurious rehab facility in the country. We send her there; they help her work through some of her shit. Best of all, you get a break from her for a few months. Let's make a list of her *issues*." Hannah made air quotes as she said issues. Then began ticking off on her fingers. "Have I got this right? Manipulative, probable narcissist. Addiction to alcohol. Addiction to spreading. Anything else?"

Scarlet blinked at her. "Um, yeah, that's a start."

"Good, let's do this thing."

"I don't think I can just let you pay for all that!"

"Scarlet;" Hannah reached across the table and took Scarlet's hand, looking into her eyes. "It was dad and his money that triggered all this shit for your mum; let me use a bit of his money to help."

"Okay," she said, stretching out the word.

"Good." Hannah smiled. "Let's make this right."

"I have to say, this is not how I was expecting my morning to go," Scarlet said.

"Me neither. I came here expecting to convince you to turn a catch up over coffee into a lunch date. More fool me, huh?"

"You're not a fool. I don't think anyone could've predicted this."

"So tell me what you know. Your mum and my dad. How did that happen?"

"She worked for him. Classic boss/secretary story

apparently, but she fell pregnant with me, and he paid her off to stop her getting in the way of his inheritance."

"Oh yeah, Grandad Hoff would skin dad alive for having an affair."

Peace washed through Scarlet for the first time in a long time. She'd resolved the problem with Rhys. She didn't need to worry about failing her course; she was taking control of the situation and withdrawing from uni. Amy was going to help her with her new career path, and she was being open and honest with her housemates about what was going on in her life. Hannah was going to help her with her mother, shoulder some of the burden, even though it wasn't her responsibility., but just because she cared.

She allowed herself to briefly indulge in a fantasy where her mother agreed to a stay in rehab. She imagined the morning where she prepared to drive her to the exclusive facility. The fantasy version of herself would consider refusing to go with Marie at the last minute, just like Marie had done when her daughter left for uni. *But I'm a better person than my mother; I wouldn't be so spiteful as to do that to her.*

Scarlet finally felt she could relax into the conversation and took another sip of her coffee. "So, tell me about this new business idea of yours."

Epilogue

"A lesbian escort agency?" The woman peered at the expensively embossed business card in her hand and then back up at Hannah. "How *novel*, Miss Hoffman."

"That's not exactly what it is." Hannah tried not to sound defensive. "We offer a companionship service exclusively for women who prefer to spend time with other women. Perhaps they're in the city on business and don't want to spend their evening alone, or they want to avoid the company of their boorish, middle-aged, male colleagues."

"You're boring me. What's your unique selling point?"

"My employees are gorgeous, well-educated, charming women." The woman gestured for Hannah to say more. "Generally, they fall on the more masculine end of the spectrum, but not always. They will behave like the perfect gentleman, if that's what the client wants. . .and if the client wants something else, well. . ." She winked.

"I have to say, I haven't heard of an agency who caters to that demographic before. Okay. Bravo." She tucked the card into her pocket, her expression as bland as ever, and turned to walk away.

"Call me if any of my *friends* can be of service, Pamela."

Hannah smiled to herself, a sense of triumph and validation filling her chest. She didn't personally need the validation, but the fact Pamela kept the card spoke volumes to her. She looked across the high-end restaurant until she spotted the table she'd come from. A petite woman with a wavy blonde bob waited for her to return. This client was paying for a "first date" experience, and she'd picked Hannah from a photo on the agency's website. The woman didn't even know that she was sitting across from the owner of the agency.

She enjoyed the freedom of it, of just being Hannah and not being Christopher Hoffman's daughter or Pamela Ng's assistant.

She slipped back into her seat with a smile.

"I'm sorry, darling, I bumped into someone I used to know coming out of the bathroom. Now, why don't you tell me something completely random about yourself?"

She leaned towards her date with an expression of interest that looked completely genuine.

"I have double-jointed thumbs. What about you, Hannah?"

"I once asked my sister out on a date. Of course, I didn't know she was my sister at the time."

"Oh my God, when did you find out?" The woman's face lit up at the scandal.

"Not straight away, but she turned down my invitation when she found out about our shared father. I found out later that was the reason why."

"It sounds like the plot of a romantic comedy."

"Well, it definitely wasn't my sister's love story."

Acknowledgments

I would like to thank everyone who provided feedback and constructive criticism throughout the writing of my first book.

The biggest thanks has to go to my editor Angelic Rodgers, who made the editing process much less daunting than I expected it to be. Thank you, Angel.

Also a special thank you to the lesfic writers community, who really are each other's biggest cheerleaders. I feel honoured to be included in your numbers.

About the Author

Emma works as a librarian. She has a degree in Criminology from the University of Brighton. As well as working in several libraries she has also worked in a warehouse, a supermarket, and a prison. She lives on the South Coast of England with her wife, daughter and their two sausage dogs. She is the 2020 Lesfic Bard Awards finalist in the category of New Author.

Emma has also written a series of educational LGBT children's books which explain how different types of families have children.

Visit Emma's website for more information about this and upcoming projects, including photos that inspired this book.

www.emmawallis.com

facebook.com/EmmaWallisAuthor

Printed in Great Britain
by Amazon